CONTROLLED
BURN

CONTROLLED BURN

BURN

ERIN SODERBERG DOWNING

SCHOLASTIC INC.

FOR MY PARENTS, KURT AND BARB SODERBERG, WHO GAVE ME A LIFE FILLED WITH OUTDOOR ADVENTURES AND TAUGHT ME TO LOVE THE WOODS.

IN MEMORY OF MY GRANDPA HOWARD, WHO DEMONSTRATED HOW TO LIVE EACH DAY TO THE FULLEST, NO MATTER THE CIRCUMSTANCES, AND HELPED ME UNCOVER THE BRAVEST AND BEST VERSION OF MYSELF.

STAGES OF A FIRE

STAGE 1: INCIPIENT (PRE-IGNITION)

When a spark or ember lands in flammable material, a fuel
source—such as dead leaves, a candlewick, or a forest full
of dry wood—sets the stage for a fire to start. In the first
stage of a fire, heat, oxygen, and fuel combine to create a
chemical reaction. Recognizing a fire at this stage provides
the best chance for suppression or escape.

CHAPTER ONE

I felt the fire before I saw it. It wasn't the suffocating heat or the smell of smoke that hit me first. Nor did I see the claws of flames that eventually reached into every corner to rip apart our lives. It's hard to explain what it means to *feel* a fire without sensing the heat of it, but that's what it was—a feeling. Maybe I noticed a change in the air, or got a weird Spidey-Sense that something was wrong? I guess I'll never know for sure.

All I *do* know for sure is, I was sitting on the couch, listening to music and thumbing through Instagram, when our house caught fire. Scrolling through my feed, I saw that a kid from my Spanish class had gotten a super-cute corgi puppy. A couple of people's stories had just reminded me it was my friend Isabel's thirteenth birthday (I quick-posted a happy birthday message, along with an old pic of the two of us from fifth-grade field day, plus hearts and a bunch of smiley faces). I'd also learned that a bunch of girls (a group I'm only sorta friends with) were out bowling together, which kind of made me jealous. A few minutes earlier, my mom had posted her Mom version of an artsy Insta picture—a glass of red wine perched beside a bright green plate loaded with grapes and cheese, all sitting atop a paperback copy of some book with a bunch of flowers on the cover.

Both my parents were out; Mom was at her book club across the street, and Dad was working at the hospital. The only things I'd been tasked with were tucking my sister, Amelia, in, convincing her to fall asleep (not the easiest job), and unloading the dishwasher. A pretty regular kind of night.

I don't know what made me pull out my headphones, but I did—and that's when I felt it. A tingling, this *feeling* that something was not quite right. I slid my phone into the front pocket of my hoodie and pulled a blanket up over my knees, listening for creaks and voices. I won't lie; I was tempted to wake my little sister, so I'd have someone to comfort me. Even though she's younger, Amelia is the brave one, and she could always figure out how to make me laugh. In times of danger, I'd much rather hide under my covers and come out when everything is marked "all clear." Besides, I've half watched enough scary movies at sleepovers to know that having a *feeling* something isn't quite right means something probably *isn't* right.

Pretty much every possible scenario passed through my head. A sudden tornado. A nest of killer spiders. An intruder lurking around the corner in the kitchen, waiting to jump out and get me. All those things terrified me, and all of them suddenly seemed very possible.

Our basement had been ripped apart for months—we were finally getting a second bathroom, and a family room with a TV and hopefully a little fridge that would have cans of soda and bottles of Gatorade. (Dad was mostly excited because we were also getting a fancy new electrical panel that would let us run the toaster *and* the coffeepot at the same time without blowing a fuse.) Just this past week, some of the guys who were working on the project had dug a big hole in the wall of our basement because of water leaking or something. So now, the only thing separating the inside from the outside was a flimsy piece of plastic that the workers taped up every night when they'd finished for the day. I suddenly realized it was entirely possible that a whole crew of bad guys—or raccoons—could easily poke through that plastic sheeting and move into our basement. I considered the fact that they could very easily be planning to take over the house and get rid of anyone in their way.

My heart beat furiously, drumming up every possible reason to be scared.

Had I known that the battery in the back hall smoke detector had been dead for years, and had I known that the construction crew unhooked the wires that connected that alarm to any other source of power, I would have had one more thing to worry about: fire. But I'd never even *thought* to worry about fire. I was scared of lots of things, but that had never been one of them.

I stood up and glanced out the front window, wishing Mom's book club would end so she would come home. But I could see a bunch of heads silhouetted behind the flimsy living room curtains at the neighbor's house, so I knew their hangout was still going strong.

That's when I smelled a faint whiff of something: a charred, smoky smell. It reminded me of the lingering smell of burned toast, but not as nice. My stomach clenched as that feeling of something-not-right intensified, and I remember I suddenly felt like I was going to be sick. I crept toward the bathroom, deliberately walking softly and slowly so as not to wake my sister.

Why didn't I run? If I'd run, the whole night might have ended differently.

Back near the bathroom, the smell of burned toast intensified. At the front of our house were the living room, kitchen, and my parents' bedroom. The bathroom was right in the middle of everything, squeezed in next to the little office where Dad had studied for his nursing school tests. At the back of the house, my room and my sister's room had once been one big room that we split into two by putting up a wall in the middle.

I raced into the bathroom and immediately threw up. My nerves do this to me a lot. When I get worked up or worried about stuff, I puke. My dad calls it a "sensitive constitution" and promises my "tender nature" will serve me well later in life. Amelia and I call it wimpiness.

After I washed my face and cleaned my mouth—*why did I take the time to brush my teeth?!*—I stepped out of the bathroom, planning to tiptoe down the hall to peek in at my sister. But as soon as I opened the bathroom door, the smoke detector started screaming at the front of the house. And now, for the first time, I felt the heat. While I'd been puking and brushing behind the closed bathroom door, a wave of intense heat had built up in the hall. Now, as I stood there in shock, it nearly knocked me off my feet.

That's when I noticed a glow coming from underneath my bedroom door.

Suddenly, I remembered my candle. The drip candle I had begged my parents to buy me for Christmas. I'd bought an antique wine jug at a neighbor's garage sale and convinced Mom and Dad to get me a collection of tall, drippy candles to use with it. My friend Anne had given me a bright rainbow candle for my birthday this past year, and Beckett had found some yummy vanilla-scented ones that were also the most amazing blue color—the same sapphire blue as my sister's eyes. As each candle burned, the wax dripped down the edges of the jar. Over the past five months I'd already built up a lovely, thick wax coat of many colors on the outside of the bottle. I'd been burning a purple candle that afternoon, while I read in my room. But I blew it out before my parents left. That was the deal—I could only burn it when I was in my room to keep an eye on it, and when one of my parents was home. I'm a rule follower; I could almost guarantee I'd blown it out before dinner. But now I wasn't so sure.

I always kept my bedroom door closed—you do that when you have a nosy little sister and too little space to call your own—so I reached out and touched the outside of my sealed door. It felt hot. I still remembered the firefighters' lesson when they visited our school in the second or third grade: Don't touch the handle or open a door if you think there's fire on the other side. Some sort of autopilot—or that Spidey-Sense again—told me *not to open the door*. My room was clearly on fire.

My room.

On fire.

I could feel my stomach rolling and heaving as I stumbled toward my sister's room. I'd left her door open a crack after I tucked her in for the night. She made me promise, so the hall light would scare any monsters away. Monsters were the only thing my sister seemed to be afraid of.

Now, just an hour after I'd snuggled with her and told her to close up her brain and shut down for the night, I pushed Amelia's bedroom door open all the way. As soon as I did, a wall of heat and smoke hit me like an ocean wave. The shock of it nearly knocked me over, but I urged myself to step forward; to get inside her room and get her out.

Go, I told myself.

Get her, my brain screamed.

Amelia! But my feet wouldn't move.

The smoke detector wailed and screamed at the front of the house, echoing my thoughts aloud.

I don't know if I'm remembering this right, but I'm pretty sure I was frozen in place for a few seconds. Flames licked at Amelia's curtains, her desk, the walls. The fire had formed a sort of yellowish-orange ring around the base of her bed.

My sister has always been a deep sleeper. She can sleep through almost anything. House-shaking thunderstorms, our neighbor's dog barking, a gas stop during road trips, even loud movies. Once, she somehow slept through a fire alarm at the hotel we were staying at on a trip to Wisconsin Dells. Someone had accidentally pulled the alarm, and everyone had to evacuate their rooms in the middle of the night. While I shuffled downstairs in my pajamas and bare feet, Mom had to carry a sleeping Amelia down six flights of stairs because she wouldn't wake up no matter how hard they shook her.

On that awful spring night, while I was the one in charge of keeping her safe, my sister must have somehow slept through the early stages of a house fire. But suddenly, someone—me, I think—was screaming. Luckily, the terrorized scream jolted Amelia awake. "Get up!" I shouted. "We have to go!"

But just as I said that, a tendril of flame danced across Amelia's litter- and laundry-strewn carpet. It caught the babyish pink bed skirt she'd been begging Dad to take off her bed for months. Fire tore at the edges of her mattress, casting her sweet face in terrifying light. She reached for me.

I screamed.

She screamed. "Maia, help me!"

I can still hear that cry, the way she wailed as the flames caught her T-shirt and ripped into her hair. Smoke filled the room, making it hard to breathe as I stared at my sister trapped inside a cage of flames.

My memory gets fuzzy after that, but later that night, someone—I'm not sure if it was Mom or Dad or one of the firefighters—told me I'd been very brave and pulled my sister to safety. I don't know how, and I don't know when I willed my feet to move, but I guess I pulled her out by the leg, maybe because it had been the only part of her body not

9

in flames. They confirmed I pulled her by the leg, because I'd somehow managed to break it during the escape.

Somehow, eventually, the flames—the ones that had tried to swallow my sister—went out.

A neighbor in back had seen the fire through our bedroom windows and called the fire department at the same time our next-door neighbor heard the smoke alarm wailing and came over to check that everything was all right. From her vantage point across the street, Mom hadn't seen a thing. Only the back half of the house had caught fire. The front looked perfectly normal—until the firefighters came in and blasted water through the entire place. I didn't get to see that part. By then, they'd loaded me into an ambulance.

Amelia and my mom were long gone, having been whisked off to the trauma center. So I rode to the hospital alone with a really nice paramedic who sang songs to keep me calm and didn't care when I puked on her shoe. Dad was waiting for me at the hospital, and he was crying, so I puked again.

Mom said it's lucky I noticed something felt wrong as early as I did. My interpretation of that comment? If I hadn't had that Spidey-Sense, my sister and I would both be dead.

But can you really call it "lucky" when your sister is knocked out in the hospital with critical burns over nearly half her body and your house is completely destroyed? And can you really call it luck—or take credit for any part of your sister's heroic rescue—when the fire was all your fault to begin with?

CHAPTER TWO

Six days after the fire that ripped up Amelia's dreams and turned our family and life into a pile of ash, Mom and I stepped off a plane directly onto the tarmac at the tiny airport in Hibbing, Minnesota. I was being shipped off to my grandparents' house for the summer, to get me out of the way while my parents tried to fix everything I broke on the night of the fire.

We hadn't visited Grandma and Grandpa at their tiny house in Thistledew, Minnesota, for more than four years. The last time we were in Minnesota, I had just turned eight, and Amelia was a few weeks shy of five. On that trip, to make the drive from Chicagoland to the middle of nowhere, Minnesota, more bearable for everyone, my parents had driven all the way through the night. My sister and I slept almost the whole time, booster seats side by side in the middle row of the minivan, while my parents traded off driving and sleeping shifts every three hours. We'd left at dinnertime, stopping for crinkly, paper-wrapped fast food burgers and chocolate milk in colorful plastic bottles. After dinner, Mom and Dad had put on a movie for us while they chatted quietly in the front seats. I woke up with the sun, and remember Mom blowing a morning kiss at me in the rearview mirror.

Life had gotten busy since then—with Amelia's gymnastics and climbing club, my soccer and babysitting, Mom's crazy caseload, and Dad's nursing school classes and now his weird and unpredictable work schedule as a newbie nurse—so we hadn't had a chance to get back to visit Thistledew again since.

Instead, Grandma Bea and Grandpa Howard came to see us once a year, looking out of place and slightly bewildered by our lives the whole time they were staying with us. Grandma puttered around the house, rearranging things Dad had just put away and asking nosy questions. Grandpa spent the whole week eating ice cream and, Amelia would say with a giggle, looking like a caged wild animal. I liked when they visited, even if they were something like strangers. But it was also sort of a relief when they left, since our lives could go back to normal. As soon as we waved goodbye, I always heard Mom let out a deep breath that I hadn't realized she'd been holding in.

Four summers and a destroyed life later, Mom and I traveled to Minnesota by plane together—just the two of us, for the first time ever. This trip, instead of burgers, we shared a big bag of trail mix. I cherry-picked all the off-brand M&M's out of the bag, but Mom didn't seem to notice that she'd been left with just stale raisins and peanuts. She didn't seem to notice *me*, either, but that was fair considering the circumstances.

On the tiny plane, there were no movies to pass the time or distract us. I just stared out the window, trying to find shapes in the fields carved into the landscape below us. I listened to the playlist my friend Anne had made me for the trip, trying not to think about how, just a week earlier,

Amelia and I had been stretched out on our backyard deck searching for shapes and stories in the clouds overhead. That day, she'd told me she was planning to become a space explorer, and she'd already started inventing a special suit that would allow her to jump out of her shuttle and hop from cloud to cloud. Amelia's plans and goals changed day by day, but they were always huge. She had no fears, and nothing could ever hold her back. Until now.

We stopped inside the terminal to get my luggage. A neighbor had given me a suitcase to use for the summer, since all of ours had burned in the fire. It was filled with clothes donated by my friends. Beckett let me take his favorite soccer jersey, which smelled like his house (and made me miss home and my friends too much, so I probably wasn't even going to wear it). I got a bunch of Anne's T-shirts and shorts and a brand-new pair of flip-flops that I knew she loved and hadn't even worn yet (she must have secretly snuck them into the pile of stuff when I wasn't looking, because I never would have taken them if I'd known); June gave me her lucky jeans (they had gotten a little too short for her, but the gift still made me feel good); and I got a couple pairs of barely worn shoes from one of my soccer teammates. I also had all new (thank goodness) underwear and socks— Dad ordered some stuff online and had it all delivered to Anne's house—to round out my summer wardrobe.

The only things from my old life that survived the fire were my phone and the clothes I was wearing that night. And—miracle of miracles—Astrid the Ostrich, who had been keeping me company on the couch while my parents were gone. I threw away all my clothes from that night; I never wanted to see them again, since they would always remind me of the worst day of my life. Astrid was the only thing I had left. She smelled like smoke and her fur was all nubby from when she got sprayed by the firefighters' hoses, but at least I had one part of my former life to carry along with me for the summer. I was hoping I could toss her in the washing machine and dryer at Grandma's, and restore her to her former fluffy glory.

While I waited for my giant, borrowed suitcase to plop onto the conveyor belt, Mom slipped away and called to check in with Dad to see how Amelia was doing. Nothing major had changed, she told me, which I guess was good news. She was still in the hospital and would be for a long time, but I guess staying the same was better than her getting worse? Everyone at the hospital kept telling me to remember that.

Outside, Grandma was waving to us from the pickup lane on the other side of the airport doors, her old tan Buick idling alongside a handful of other cars. She looked just like I remembered. Her hair was cut short, like Mom's, but it was much messier. Unlike me and Mom, Grandma Bea had hair that had faded from chestnut brown to a pure, snowy white. Everything about the way Grandma carried herself screamed No Nonsense, just like Mom, but in a totally different way. My grandma wore an embroidered sweatshirt, jeans that looked like they'd been around for years and had at least another century left in them, and not one spot of jewelry or makeup. Mom wasn't high-maintenance, at all, but she never went anywhere without a perfectly coordinated outfit and simple but elegant jewelry, and her face and body language oozed the kind of confidence that made her look like the sort of person you didn't want to mess with.

When we got to the car, Mom offered to drive home from the airport, but Grandma looked at her like she was crazy. "Think I'm too old to drive?" she asked, lifting her thin, almost-invisible eyebrows.

Mom sighed. I waited for her to say something funny in response, but instead she just slid into the back seat and motioned for me to take the front. I hadn't even called shotgun. Amelia and I had a running game of shotgun, even though she was both too young and too short to ever actually *sit* in the front seat (my parents had just deemed *me* tall enough, finally), she liked to see who could call dibs first whenever we got outside. She almost always won.

Grandma and I talked about school while she drove along the desolate backcountry road that led to my new home for the summer. This time, it would be *me* feeling out of place in *their* home. I stared out the window and tried to imagine what a few months spent in the middle of nowhere would be like. Grandpa liked to hunt; what if I was forced to eat deer meat? When they visited, Grandma always made this stew that had unidentifiable chunks of something meat-like that managed to be both chewy *and* stringy. Maybe now was a good time to become a vegetarian like Beckett's family?

Would Grandma and Grandpa ever know if I'd decided last-minute to be a vegetarian of convenience?

How much did Grandma and Grandpa *actually* know about me, anyway? Could I trick them into thinking I was someone totally different from the girl I was at home? Maybe here, in Thistledew, I could be Maia the Brave. Maia the Fearless. Maia the Magnificent. Maia, who never let anyone down and didn't almost kill her own sister.

I stared out the car window at the trees whizzing by. In the distance, a giant metal tower rose up above the tree line. Back home, the Chicago skyline was huge, colorful, shiny, and one of my favorite sights on earth. This single, spindly tower rising up above the never-ending forest was the closest thing to a skyline for hundreds of miles. "What's that?" I asked, pointing.

"The fire tower," Grandma Bea said.

I closed my eyes and tried to unsee it. In the back seat, I heard Mom suck in a breath through her teeth, but she remained silent. It already felt like I was all on my own here in Minnesota, in this strange place with almost-strangers. Mom's head and heart were obviously already back in Chicago with my dad and sister—which was where she belonged. Me? I belonged here, banished to a place where I could do no further harm.

"Do you know, the town was built around that tower?" Grandma asked, gesturing at it with her chin. I couldn't tell if she'd noticed me tense up at the word *fire*, or if she'd heard the first sound Mom had made since we'd left the airport. I'm sure she could guess it wasn't anyone's favorite subject at the moment.

"I didn't know that," I said quietly.

"Rumor has it," she said, glancing at me, "some folks at the Forest Service were looking for a good spot to set up a tower to keep watch for forest fires. They just kept moving through the forest, until one of them guys stopped and said: 'You know what? This'll do.'"

I stared out at that tower, looming over everything. Looking out, keeping watch. Climbing up above the treetops, into the wind and rain and lightning. To climb it, you would have to force yourself to trust a rickety old structure that could collapse at any second. My stomach turned at the thought. I rolled down my window a tiny bit, to get some fresh air.

"Get it?" Grandma Bea asked, glancing at me. "This'll do? Thistledew."

"Oh." I choked out something that sounded like a laugh. "Yeah."

A population sign marked the edge of town: THISTLEDEW POP. 500.

"Five hundred people exactly?" I asked.

"Nah," Grandma said, slowing to a crawl as we drove into town. "Five hundred, more or less. People die, a few are born each year. No one wants to admit we're smaller than five hundred nowadays. Not worth making a new sign."

As we drove through town, I took stock of the businesses that lined Main Street (the main street through town was actually *called* Main Street, which I found satisfying). There was a bank, a small grocery store, a café, three different bar/restaurants, two gas stations (one on each end of town), a hardware store, and an antique shop. It had to be the most clichéd and old-fashioned small town in the history of small towns.

"Nothing's changed," Mom muttered, finally speaking for the first time in nearly an hour. I'd started to wonder if she'd forgotten we were in the car with her. "Maia, this place looks exactly like it did when I was a kid."

"Oh," I said, turning to flash her a smile, encouraging her to keep talking, to tell me more. "That's cool."

"The penny candy at the Y Store went up to a dime apiece," Grandma told her in a stiff voice. "So some things have changed."

"Are you still working there, Ma?" Mom asked.

"Most days," Grandma Bea said, pointing at the enormous, brightly lit gas station at the edge of town. "Maia, that's the Y Store. Where I work as a cashier."

"Why are there two gas stations in a town this small?" I wondered aloud. "Is there a difference between them?"

"Gas is three cents cheaper on this end of town, and we sell ice cream cones. Al's Service Shop on the other end of town has a slushy machine and free air."

"Free air?" I turned and watched town disappear out the back window of the car. We'd driven the entire length of it in less than thirty seconds.

"For tires," Grandma told me, making a sound with her tongue that suggested I should have known that already.

Grandma Bea veered off Main Street, just past the Y Store. The only thing I could remember about their house from our last visit was that it sat at the very end of town, on the very end of a dead-end road. Grandma Bea and Grandpa Howard's place was literally the last house in Thistledew proper. It marked the end of the road, in a town Dad had told me was nicknamed "The End of the Road." This was the last town for miles. Beyond Thistledew, there was nothing but the wild forest and lakes that made up the Boundary Waters Canoe Area Wilderness, which led directly into the Quetico Provincial Park in Canada. We were as much in the middle of nowhere as one could possibly be, and a part of me was grateful for the escape.

The old Buick rambled down the rocky road my grandparents lived on. There were two other houses on this short spur of road that forked off Main Street. The three houses were spaced pretty far apart, but they all shared one big yard. Unlike our neighborhood, there were no fences or hedges to mark where one property ended and another began. "I hope you like your neighbors," I said, just to say something. Mom had disappeared back into her silence.

Grandma grunted. I wasn't sure if that was a yes or a no.

The house next to my grandparents' house looked abandoned—the grass was long, and there was a faded FOR SALE sign leaning against the crumbling front steps. The only sign of life was a pot of dead flowers on the bottom step. "Where did Mrs. Myntie go?" my mom asked. I turned around to look at her, realizing I only had one more day to see her face in person before she abandoned me here. Mom was pointing to the empty-looking house. "Did she move?"

"She died," Grandma said bluntly. "'Bout a year or so ago. No one's bought the house yet."

Mom opened her mouth, as if she wanted to say something, but then she closed it again. I heard her sniffle, and I realized she was crying. Probably about Mrs. Myntie being dead. Her emotions, usually very much under control, had been pretty messed up since the fire.

Grandma pulled into her driveway and turned off the car. None of us moved to get out. The car clicked as it cooled in the still afternoon air. Finally, Mom opened her door with a sigh. She grabbed her backpack off the seat next to her and trudged inside the house, leaving me to handle my suitcase full of borrowed clothes by myself. I know she was distracted by everything happening with Amelia, so she probably forgot I had stuff that needed to get inside the house, too.

Part of *me* hoped she had conveniently forgotten all about my bag because a part of *her* didn't want to leave me here alone with these strange old people.

I wondered if she was at all sad to say goodbye and leave me for the summer.

I wondered if she realized I was the one who'd destroyed our lives and our home.

I wondered if she blamed me.

I wondered if I'd ever get my life back.

But more than anything, I wondered: When would I be allowed to go home again?

CHAPTER THREE

As I tugged my stuff out of the car, I heard the distinctive pop and growl of a vehicle driving down the gravel road toward the house. I turned, and there was Grandpa Howard sitting astride a massive motorcycle. He pulled off his helmet and we stared at each other for an awkward few moments. It's not every day you see your seventy-year-old grandfather riding a motorcycle.

"Hi, Pops," I finally said.

"Kid," he replied.

"That your usual ride?" I asked, grunting as I heaved the suitcase halfway out of the trunk.

"Yup."

"Is it scary? Riding without a roof or a seat belt or anything?"

He didn't reply, just toed down the little kickstand to park his cycle at the end of the unpaved driveway.

"Is it called a kickstand when it's on a motorcycle? Or is that just bikes?"

He chuckled. "How many questions are gonna spill out of that mouth of yours?"

"Sorry," I muttered. I gave my suitcase one hard, final tug and it spilled out of the trunk and onto my foot. The corner landed squarely on my little toe, sending a blast of pain up the outside of my foot. Shoving the suitcase aside, I hopped on the other foot, hooting and whooping with pain. "Ow ow ow ow." It was shocking how much you could feel in a single little toe.

Tears sprang to my eyes and I glanced at Grandpa to see if he'd noticed. Before they could roll down my cheeks, I blinked them away, remembering how much Amelia must hurt, with burns covering half her body. It must feel like this, times a million. At least the doctors were keeping her pumped full of sedatives and medicine to stop her from hurting too much. Hopefully she couldn't feel her scorched and peeling skin, or the tubes that fed food and fluids and fresh air into her damaged body. I had no right to whine about my wounded toe, even if it didn't feel great.

Grandpa Howard leaned against his motorcycle, obviously not in any kind of hurry to help me out.

"Don't worry, I'm okay," I grumbled. "I think I broke my toe, but I've got it."

"Want me to cut it off?" he asked. "Then it won't hurt anymore."

I think he was kidding.

As I dragged my suitcase across the gravel, I tried to ignore the throbbing by changing the subject. "You couldn't pay me to get on the back of a motorcycle. Do you know how many accidents there are involving those things?"

Grandpa didn't respond. He just strapped his helmet into a little case on the back of the cycle and followed me silently into the house. As soon as I opened the front door, I remembered what my grandparents' life smelled like: a combination of homemade soup, cut grass, and a sort of earthy smell that I think seeped up from the unfinished—and exceedingly creepy—basement. It had been years since I'd been inside this house, but the smell was instantly familiar.

I heaved my suitcase up the dirty entryway stairs and into the kitchen. Mom and Grandma were sitting at the table. Grandma was watching Mom, who was focused on her phone with an untouched cup of coffee in front of her.

"How's Amelia?" I asked, for about the tenth time that day. I sat down at the table and peeled off my sock to check my toe. It was sort of greenish yellow, and at least twice the size of the toe next to it. Most likely broken. I'd have to go to the hospital. Was there even a hospital anywhere near here? I decided I'd wait to say anything until tomorrow when Mom was gone. She didn't need to worry about my baby toe when she had my baby sister's entire life to think about.

"She's the same," Mom said, without looking at me.

Grandma smiled at me. "Do you want something to drink? A snack?" That's when she noticed my bag and said, "Or I guess maybe you want to unpack first?"

"Yeah, that would be great," I said, but didn't really mean it. What I really wanted was to put my suitcase back in the trunk and drive right back to the airport with Mom, to return to my sister and home and be *there* for my family. Not here.

Grandma pointed to a door right off the kitchen. "That's

the guest room. It's all yours for the summer. I put fresh sheets on the pullout bed and emptied a few of the shelves in the closet. Make yourself at home."

"Okay, thanks," I said.

Home. This wasn't home. It would never be home. But I had to pretend it was, at least until my family was willing to let me come back. I'd tried to tell my parents that I *had* to stay in Chicago; that Amelia would need me while she was healing. Even if she was totally knocked out so her body had freedom to focus on keeping her system alive, she would *know* if I was there or not.

But with no house to live in, and my sister sleeping away the last weeks of school and her summer vacation in a hospital bed, my parents decided it would be best for everyone if I went far, far away for a while. I knew I deserved this punishment, especially since I was the only one to blame for our lives imploding, but it still hurt. It wasn't clear exactly how long I'd be banished, but I hoped it wouldn't be more than a few weeks.

Even though grades and test scores and homework mattered in middle school, Dad convinced my teachers to let me skip the last few weeks of the quarter without any drama. I checked the student portal and saw that every single teacher had given me pity As on all my remaining assignments for the year. Anne would be jealous I got to skip the end-of-year project in World Studies—especially since we were planning to be partners for it. That is, she'd be jealous until she remembered the reason why I got a free pass.

As I limped toward the guest bedroom, my mom called out, "Hey, Maia?"

I turned. Besides seeing my sister and home restored to normal, there was nothing I wanted more than for my mom to pull me into her lap, wrap her warm arms around me, and promise me that everything would be okay. That I wouldn't hurt much longer. But instead, she said, "Looks like I can catch a flight back to Chicago tonight. I'd have to connect in Minneapolis, but I'd like to switch my flight, if you think you're all set here?"

No, I'm not all set.

No, I don't want you to leave.

No, please stay with me, for one more night at least.

"That's fine," I lied. "I'll be fine."

CHAPTER FOUR

Less than an hour later, Grandma drove Mom back to the airport so she would be there in time for the next flight out. Grandpa and I were left alone, to figure out dinner and each other.

"So . . ." I said, propping my chin in my hands at the kitchen table. My toe was throbbing, and I was nervous, but I offered Grandpa a fake smile to try to make both of us less uncomfortable. This was weird. I hadn't been alone with Grandpa Howard in a long time—maybe ever. "What's your plan for tonight?"

"Hungry?" he asked.

"I could eat," I said.

"Feel like ice cream?"

"For dinner?"

"Would you prefer I prepare you a beef tenderloin, Your Majesty?"

I giggled. I guess it was the image of my gruff grandpa— in his wool pants and plaid flannel—whipping up some sort of fussy dinner. I pictured us sitting at a candlelit table together, cloth napkins and everything. "Ice cream would be great," I said.

"Pick your toppings," he said, gesturing to a cabinet above the sink. I stood up to see what the options were. At the front of the cabinet, there was a plastic basket filled with individual pouches of caramel, chocolate, and butterscotch sauce. There were also little containers of sprinkles—chocolate, rainbow, and candy snowflakes. I moved the basket to the table just as Grandpa dropped two big bowls, two plastic tubs of ice cream, and a can of whipped cream on the table. "Get spoons," he ordered.

I did as I was told, then we both loaded up our bowls. I watched, fascinated, as Grandpa Howard built an elaborate sundae, complete with a small army of sprinkles.

"Bon appétit," I said, holding my spoon up in the air.

"Don't tell your mom this was dinner," he said, glancing sideways at me.

"Deal."

We ate in silence, then Grandpa washed our dishes and gently nestled our clean bowls in the dish drying rack.

"Hey, Pops?" I said.

He grunted, which—I guess—was his way of saying, "Yeah?"

"Remember when I dropped the suitcase on my toe? It still hurts really bad. Do you think you could maybe take me to the doctor tomorrow so they can see if it's broken?"

"Just the toe, eh?"

"My little one." I began to peel off my sock, propping the wounded foot up on my other knee. "See? It's all yellow and green and funny-looking. I might need a cast or something."

Grandpa eyed me from across the kitchen. "A cast. For your toe?"

"Yeah?" I said.

Then Grandpa began to laugh. "You're gonna need to deal with it, kid. If it hurts so bad that you want to waste good money on a doctor who will tell you to tape it up and give it time, I can cut it off. That's going to be easier and cheaper in the long run."

It suddenly felt like my delicious sundae dinner was about to come right back up and land on the ugly green kitchen floor. Grandpa must have sensed he'd gone too far, because a moment later his face sort of crumpled and he said, "What I'm trying to say is, there's nothing they can do for a wounded pinkie toe. I'll grab some tape and we can fix it to its neighbor. That should help keep it stable, anyway. Might hurt a little less if it has company holding it up."

I nodded. While Grandpa got the tape and some scissors, I tried to keep myself from crying. He cradled my foot on his lap and gently taped my ugly, bruised little toe to the one next to it. "Better?" he asked roughly, packing up the first aid supplies.

"Yeah," I whispered, because it did feel a little better. I guess, deep down, I kind of knew there wasn't much that a doctor or anyone could do for an injured little toe. But it hurt, and I wanted someone to tell me how long until the pain would go away. I wanted someone to patch it up for me and tell me it wasn't broken. I wanted those answers about my life, too. Would *that* pain ever go away, or would our family be broken forever?

The doctor who'd checked me over the night of the fire had made me talk to a hospital therapist. "Doctor Dan" stopped by my room sometime the next morning, right after a lady from the fire department—an *arson investigator*, I think she'd called herself—had come by to ask me a bunch of questions about what I could remember from the fire. I didn't want to talk to the therapist any more than I wanted to talk to an arson investigator, but a nurse who'd been keeping an eye on me all night told me it would help to talk things out with someone who could help me sort through stuff. But Doctor Dan hadn't helped at all; he just nodded and told me he understood my pain. There was no *way* he could understand. He kept wanting me to talk about my feelings and fears, but I wasn't going to tell some stranger all my secrets. I couldn't tell anyone about my candle, certainly not Doctor Dan. If he—or anyone—knew I was the person who was responsible for the fire, would I be arrested? Hadn't I already been punished enough?

I slipped my sock and shoe back on and followed Grandpa outside. He hadn't told me to follow him, and I wasn't even sure he really wanted me there, but I wasn't ready to be alone in that unfamiliar house. Besides, I'd been cooped up in a plane and the car all day, and my lungs were screaming for fresh air. I'd been having a hard time getting a good, full breath since the fire—I'd inhaled more than a healthy amount of smoke that night—and the cool, woodsy air smelled sweet and refreshing. I took a deep breath, closed my eyes, and let it out slowly.

I kept my eyes closed and just breathed until, suddenly,

I felt something bump against my thigh. It was a dog—a big, dark, mangy mess of a dog with a giant snout, soft chocolate-brown eyes, and a huge black nose. "Hey," I whispered, reaching out a hand to let it sniff me. It almost looked like a tiny bear with skinny legs.

The dog nosed my arm, pushing my hand up to scratch its ears.

"Who's this?" I called out to Grandpa. He was puttering around doing something in the yard.

"Don't have a name," he said, scowling at the dog.

"Whose dog is it?" I asked, getting down on my knees. The dog pushed its big snout against my stomach, then rubbed its head against me.

"Don't know," Grandpa said unhelpfully.

"Where did it come from?" I asked, fully aware that I was annoying him with my incessant questions again.

"It just turned up one day, looking for food. Guessing some jerk abandoned it on the side of the highway." He pointed to a small doghouse in the back corner of the yard. "Sleeps there."

I coughed as the dog shoved me over, trying and failing to get its whole body on my lap. "This dog," I called out, "sleeps in a doghouse in your yard?"

"That's what I just said."

I snorted out a laugh. "But it's not *your* dog?"

"Exactly."

"Do you feed it?"

Grandpa narrowed his eyes at me. "I leave some food and

water out, if that's what you're asking. It's there if he's hungry."

I was starting to get the sense Grandpa was a reluctant softie. "So you feed him, and he sleeps here . . . but you won't admit he's your dog?"

"I don't want a dog. They just take up space and don't make much sense, if you ask me."

The dog sneezed, then farted— loud. The sound of his own fart startled the mutt, who jumped and spun in a quick circle as if to say: "Who did that?! *En gurde!*"

I was in love. "Can I name him?"

"Fine by me," Grandpa said. "Teach him a few commands and see if you can make the thing useful. If he starts doing anything more than just begging for food and digging up my gardens, I might consider letting him in the house come winter. But if you wanna know the truth, I'm hoping that thing wanders off before it comes to that."

I looked over to see if he was serious. I think what he'd just said was, if I trained the dog and made Grandpa fall in love, the pup would get to stay and call this home. Challenge accepted. Based on how cuddly the big beast was with *me*, a brand-new friend, I didn't expect he was going to wander off anytime soon—he obviously loved people and wanted to be around them. Which meant I needed to help this furry guy earn his ticket inside.

What I hadn't noticed while playing with the dog was that Grandpa had set to work prepping a small bonfire to clear up some brush and sticks from the yard. He flicked a match, and I could see the spark catch, swallow up a strip of bark, and lick at the surrounding twigs. The crackling sound made my heart race as the fire took hold and my body immediately flew back to that night. I saw the fire reaching out of the firepit to crawl across the dry yard, catching leaves, swallowing up sticks, and coming for the house and trees overhead. I had to get away; I didn't want to smell it or see it, so I went around to the front of the house. The dog trailed after me. "We need to pick a name for you," I told the beast, once we were safely out of the fire line.

He wagged his tail and—I swear it's the truth—smiled at me.

Together, the dog and I wandered to the end of the driveway and turned toward town. I figured I was safe roaming in a place with only five hundred people (more or less). And Grandpa didn't seem too worried about my health and well-being. So, I set off to explore.

Just past the late Mrs. Myntie's house, the third and last house on the block was small and charming. It had cute gingerbread-house-looking trim and was painted a fun pale-purple color. It reminded me of Amelia's dollhouse, the one in her room that had burned in the fire, along with all her other worldly possessions—a miniature house fire within the giant fire.

My sister's dollhouse wasn't exactly a *doll*house, but more a place to collect odds and ends from her life. For a long time, there were no actual dolls inside, just random rock monsters and sock puppets and LEGO figures. Amelia claimed that regular dollhouse figurines were all sorts of creepy. Last Christmas, I wrapped up my whole collection of movie POP! figures so that Olaf, Moana, Shrek, and a bunch of Minions could fill the dollhouse with more life and fun. She'd been so excited about the gift that she had tackled me off the couch and onto the floor, breaking Mom's favorite coffee mug in the scuffle. That was Amelia—so full of excitement and life and *oomph* that sometimes her energy just sort of exploded out of her.

I shook my head, willing myself to stop thinking about my sister, since even the best memories made me sad. I began to obsess about how she was doing, and wonder if she could feel or remember anything. I wished I knew what Dad was doing while he sat by her bedside. I wondered if he'd had any time to think about me and consider the fact that it was my fault we were all in this mess. It was *my* fault she'd almost died, *my* fault our house had caught on fire, *my* fault I hadn't gotten her out sooner, and *my* fault I'd been sent away from my family.

I took another look at the cute purple house and noticed that there was a jungle gym in the backyard, which suggested kids might live there. There were also no fewer than thirty giant cardboard boxes stacked up along the side of the house. I hadn't noticed those when we drove into town a few hours earlier, but I guess I hadn't really been paying attention.

As we walked past the life-sized gingerbread house, my new dog pal began wagging his tail. He trotted up the driveway and lifted his leg to pee on one of the boxes. "No!" I called out. Obviously, Lesson One in our training program would need to be: Don't pee on personal property.

"That's his favorite pee spot," a little voice said. I noticed a pair of eyes peeking out at me from two holes cut out of the side of one of the boxes. "I really don't mind. If he needs to pee on my house to feel like he's welcome here, that's fine by me. It's what dogs do."

I made my way toward the pile of boxes. As soon as I was close, a small, fluffy head popped out of the top of the box and fixed me with a big, toothless grin. "Hello."

"Hello, yourself," I said, studying the kid. He looked maybe seven or eight and had messy light brown hair and a round, friendly face that reminded me a little bit of a teddy bear from Build-A-Bear Workshop. "You know this dog?"

"Sure. We're neighbors," said the kid. "He pees on my fort, I feed him ham from my lunch." He heaved a sigh and explained, "My mom packs me a ham and butter sandwich for school *every single day*, but I don't like ham. I've told her a thousand times that I want just plain ol' butter. But Mom keeps sneaking in ham, thinking I won't notice or something. So I just peel it off the bread on my way to the bus each morning and feed it to Big Bear. Works out pretty good for both of us."

I laughed. He was a cute kid. "Big Bear, huh? That's a good name."

"Really? You like it?" the kid said, his eyes wide. "I think it suits him."

"Me too. So, is that the dog's name?"

"He doesn't have a collar," the kid said. "I don't know his real name."

"Big Bear feels like a good fit," I said with a shrug. I glanced down at the dog, who wagged in agreement. "And I think he likes it—maybe we can call him Bear for short, so he doesn't get a complex about his size. But he does look like a bear, kinda." I didn't tell the kid that's sort of what *he* looked like, too. "What's your name?"

"Griffin." The kid extended his hand and I shook it. It was sticky and sort of wet, but it didn't bother me. He was someone to talk to, and I couldn't really afford to be picky. Grandpa wasn't much of a chatter, my friends were thousands of miles away, and I desperately missed Amelia's constant conversation. "I'm nine," Griffin announced. "Just about to finish third grade, so I'd say congratulations are in order. Who are you?"

"Maia. I'll be thirteen next September, and . . . I guess I'm done with sixth grade?" That felt weird to say—that I was done with sixth grade. I hadn't gotten to do any of the regular last-day-of-school stuff, hadn't taken my math final exam, didn't even get to clear out my locker. I was at school with all my friends one day, and gone the next. Just like I had a comfy house one day, a hospital bed the next. Had a cheerful, full-of-ideas, fearless little sister one day, and a family living minute-to-minute in the intensive care burn unit the next. I felt my stomach churning and turned my attention back to Griffin. "My grandparents live down

35

the road. I'm going to be staying with them for a while."

Griffin's eyes widened. Based on his expression, I had a feeling he knew my story. "Oh."

"Yeah," I said, reaching down to give the dog a pat. "Oh."

After a beat, Griffin grinned again. "Let's be friends. Want a tour?"

I shrugged. "Sure."

He ushered me into his fort, carefully avoiding Big Bear's pee-soaked corner. What had looked like nothing more than a messy pile of boxes from the outside turned out to be an epic fort inside. Griffin had filled his cardboard space with toys, comic books, and a few battery-powered lanterns, using duct tape and sticks to connect and stack the collection of boxes into a tiny fortress. I had to duck and crawl through the labyrinth of tunnels, but it was worth it. The kid had serious fort-making talent.

After he'd led me into each cardboard room, hastily describing the intended purpose of each wing of the fort—snack space, battle prep zone, nap nest, and the LEGO building box—we slithered into a larger space stuffed full of musty outdoor pillows and a few ratty blankets. Griffin settled down on a blanket and opened a spiral-bound book.

"What do you know about fishing?" he asked me, opening to a random page.

"Not much," I confessed.

He leafed through the book, then looked up hopefully. "Forensics?"

I cringed. "Nothing."

"Mbiras or sistrums?" he said, flipping to another page.

I lifted my eyebrows. "I don't even know what those words mean. Why?"

Griffin pushed the book into my lap. "I'm trying to earn every single one of the Bear Scout badges this summer, before Scouts starts up again in the fall. Wanna help?"

"Do I need to be an expert in something?"

Griffin's eyes lit up. "*Are* you an expert in something?"

"No."

He sighed, then shrugged. "Well, that's okay, I guess. We can learn together." He thrust his hand out toward me, and we shook again. "It's a deal. We're a team now. Except I can't pay you or anything, and I get to keep all the badges, since you don't have a Scouts shirt. You *don't* have a Scouts shirt, right?"

"No Scouts shirt," I confirmed. "The badges can be all yours. And no payment is necessary. I'm happy to help." As soon as I said it, I realized it was true. Because now I had a plan to survive this summer in Thistledew, even if everything I truly cared about was thousands of miles away.

While my sister healed, I would help Griffin get his Scout badges, teach a stray dog a few tricks, and do everything in my power to try to earn the right to come home. Any other summer, that wouldn't have sounded too shabby. But this summer, when all I really wanted was to get my sister and my life back *now*, all I could tell myself was, "This'll do."

STAGES OF A FIRE

STAGE 2: FLASHOVER (FLAMING)

In the flashover stage, the mix of heat, oxygen, and fuel increases the odds of a fire growing and building. If not suppressed, the fire begins to spread beyond the initial ignition point to consume additional fuel sources. Flames are visible and gaining ground. It is during this stage when a deadly "flashover" can occur, potentially trapping, injuring, or killing anyone caught in the flames.

CHAPTER FIVE

I lay awake in bed for hours that first night at Grandma Bea and Grandpa Howard's house, listening to a symphony of unfamiliar sounds. This far outside civilization, nighttime wasn't the same. Each noise was magnified, the sounds of darkness amplified by surrounding quiet.

The ticking of the clock in the corner of the living room wasn't something I'd noticed in the daytime, but as soon as the rest of the house was put to bed, it ticked and tocked away the seconds, reminding me with each shift of the hands that I couldn't fall asleep, wouldn't fall asleep, really wanted to sleep. The hum of the baseboard heater that ran along the bottom of the wall revved and groaned like a tiny motorboat crossing the carpeted den. Out in the kitchen, the ancient fridge clicked on and off, sounding far too much like the tap of tentative footsteps outside my makeshift bedroom.

Trembling, I hugged Astrid the Ostrich tight, hoping something familiar from home might bring back enough peaceful memories to protect me from this scary new place. But despite the fact that Grandma had washed and dried her—with a bonus dryer sheet thrown in for good measure—Astrid still smelled faintly of smoke, like a nightmare, which was not what she was supposed to smell like. She was supposed to offer the comfort I needed.

I shoved my beloved ostrich away, scrambled out of the

pull-out bed, and plugged in the night-light Grandma had set out for me, "just in case." As soon as I jammed it into the outlet, the world of my bedroom was bathed in an eerie blue light. For a moment, the murky blue tricked me into thinking I was trapped underwater. My breath caught in my throat, choking me, until I remembered I could still breathe, that I was perfectly safe and could take a deep breath whenever I needed it.

There had been quite a few times this past week when I'd had trouble catching my breath and felt panic racing through my body as I fought for air. Both Amelia and I had sucked in a lot of smoke and fumes and other bad stuff during the fire, and even though I hadn't needed a breathing tube like my sister, Dad told me it would take time for my body and lungs to return to normal. I had a feeling that even if my lungs eventually *did* go back to normal, the rest of me never would. Not quite.

I'd always been scared of all kinds of semi-normal things: tall buildings, slipping down the stairs, getting sucked underwater and not being able to figure out which way was up. One day last summer, when a bunch of my friends took turns riding the zip line into the water at the outdoor pool near my house, I'd offered to take pictures so I didn't have to do it—because I knew I'd be too scared to jump into the pool when I reached the end of the ride, and then maybe the zip line wouldn't stop the way it was supposed to, and I'd smash right into the concrete on the other side of the pool. My friends all knew me well enough that they understood what I was doing, even without me saying anything out loud. I was pretty sure heights, falling, drowning, and zip-lining were all valid fears.

But now, I was suddenly afraid of absolutely everything, valid and not. During the past week, I'd noticed dozens of new fears wiggling into my brain: the shapeless dark, intruders, choking on my chewing gum, getting hit by a car, falling off my bike, and a whole collection of illnesses and conditions that I'd overheard people talking about after the fire, while I was resting at the hospital. Since arriving in Minnesota, I was now also terrified something awful would happen to Big Bear during the night. Each day, the fears seemed to multiply.

I thought of that night again and wondered for the millionth time this week: If I hadn't let my fear take over on the night of the accident, would my sister still be in the hospital? I had gone into the bathroom to puke, and then I'd stood in Amelia's doorway for I don't know how long, watching silently as my sister got consumed and swallowed up by the fire. I could have been so much quicker if I hadn't been so scared.

I would never forgive myself. But maybe I could try to be less scared from now on, so my fears could never cripple me like that again.

As I lay there in the darkness, I promised myself that tomorrow would be a new day. I couldn't keep letting these irrational what-ifs take over. I was pretty sure that Mom and Dad had sent me away for the summer because dealing with me and my problems and everything I was afraid of was just too much—especially when they had something serious and real, like Amelia's injuries, to cope with. They didn't need to say it for me to know: My sister had real problems; mine were just in my head.

But if I could prove to my parents that I was strong, and capable, and able to take care of myself, they might let me come home soon. They might let me try to help fix the things I'd broken. If I didn't need so much fixing myself, I wouldn't be in the way.

With the darkness now pushed to the shadows, everything inside my little den looked like it was glowing. For the first time, I noticed there was a giant stuffed bumblebee hanging, like a hunter's stuffed prize, in the corner of the room. Its enormous checkerboard eyes stared at me, daring me to nod off so it could sink down and sting me to death. I stared back at it, reminding myself that it was harmless—a silly, stuffed, incredibly lifelike King Kong of a bee. Still, that bee glared at me in the midnight haze. I reached down and pulled the night-light back out of the wall, deciding that the mystery of the dark unknown was better than being able to see everything there was to be afraid of.

I pushed open the window over my bed, desperate for fresh air, then flopped back down in bed and begged my body to go to sleep. Something hooted in a tree outside while another creature rustled and snuffed in the leaves below my window.

Just an owl, I told myself.

"A squirrel or Big Bear," I whispered aloud, over and over again.

Way across the yard, I could hear the far-off crackle of Grandpa's campfire. While I was getting ready for bed, I'd learned that most nights, Grandpa slept by himself out in an old pull-behind camper he and Grandma kept parked in the yard behind the house. This habit seemed weird to me, but so did Grandpa. Maybe it was perfectly normal for someone like him to sleep in a camper alone in the yard. It made me sad to think of Grandma crawling into her big bed by herself every night, but maybe she liked the peace and quiet.

Maybe no one else was like Amelia and me, sisters who looked forward to our Saturday-night sleepovers. Almost every weekend, my sister would drag her sleeping bag into my bedroom and camp out on the floor next to my bed. Eventually, she'd slither up into bed right beside me and we'd tell each other stories until I could sense her voice getting husky and sleepy and could see her eyes drifting closed, even though she never wanted to be the first one to fall asleep.

Outside, Grandpa Howard's fire clicked and popped, and I could imagine the embers glowing orange, tendrils of smoke curling up toward the sky. I suddenly felt like I was going to be sick, so I scrambled up to my knees and slid the window closed, focusing instead on the nervous tick of the clock.

I missed my sister. I wondered what—if anything—she

could hear from her hospital bed. Would Mom be sitting beside her wrapped body, watching cooking shows on the tiny TV perched on the little shelf above Amelia's feet? Were there still machines that beeped and ticked behind her all night, like Grandma's clock? Could she hear the chatter at the nurses' station, and was she making mental notes of the funny conversations she overheard so she could tell me all of them when she came home?

Could you hear things when you were that out of it? She was still so drugged up, it was almost like she was in a medically induced coma, Mom told me. So she probably wasn't aware of much going on. If I were there and could read to her, would she be able to follow along in the story? Had she noticed that I wasn't coming by anymore? Was she scared of what was happening? Did it hurt? Would she come home? And would there ever *be* a home for us again?

The questions and the darkness pressed down, choking me, daring me to breathe. If my sister were there, the strange sounds of this unfamiliar place would be muffled by her tiny, breathy snores. Her little arm would flop over me, hugging me in the dark. I had always hated the way she loved to sleep uncomfortably close. But right now, I'd give anything to have her soft, skinny arm trapping me under Grandma's scratchy blankets. To hear the rhythm of her snores, to feel her furnace of a body curled against me, and her hot nighttime breath on my neck.

But Amelia was miles away. No one could touch her. And

the secret keeping me from falling asleep was, it was all my fault.

All my fault.

All my fault.

I had never felt so helpless or alone.

CHAPTER SIX

The next morning, I woke to the sound of dishes clanking on the other side of the den door. It was still hazy outside in the early morning, and I was not ready to be up. But I was a guest, operating on someone else's rules and schedule, so I dragged myself out of bed and tumbled into the kitchen. "G'morning," I muttered, rubbing my eyes.

Grandma Bea was standing at the stove, frying eggs. Grandpa Howard was sitting at the table, eating eggs. "Hungry?" Grandma asked.

I realized I was starving. Delicious as the ice cream had been the night before, it hadn't stuck the way a real meal would have. "Sure," I said. "But I can make something for myself."

Grandma gave me a look that told me to zip it. So I sat down next to Grandpa, waiting to be served. It was kind of nice, actually. Most mornings before school, I was the one helping my sister get her breakfast. I'd carefully pour Amelia's cereal (she didn't like when any of the crumbs from the bottom of the box made their way into her bowl) and get her a glass of juice, and then we'd sit and read our books while we ate breakfast together, just the two of us.

Dad used to be around in the mornings, but after he started nursing school and I was old enough to be left home alone with my sister, Dad's schedule turned into a mess. He had classes, and went to the library to study a *lot*, and he had also picked up a job helping out at a nursing home to make ends meet. Mom's job as a lawyer—the boring kind, not the stand up and shout and perform in a courtroom kind—meant she was out of the house and at work by seven most days.

A few moments after I settled in at the table, Grandma slid a plate of eggs and toast toward me. Then she perched in the seat beside me, no plate of eggs for herself, and looked at me. I pretended I didn't notice her staring. It was kind of weird, having someone watch you eat over-easy eggs.

"Would you like to take a trip to the lake today?" she asked me finally. "It's supposed to be warm, so maybe you'd like to swim?"

"Maybe," I said. I wasn't a good swimmer—deep water was one of the many things that terrified me, even before the fire—but I didn't want to start blurting out my fears on day one. New Maia didn't do that, I reminded myself; Maia the Brave wasn't allowed to *have* fears.

"We go to church at nine on Sundays," she said, after another long silence. "Do you have anything nice to wear?"

I swallowed a big bite of egg, mentally rummaging through the collection of borrowed and donated clothes in my suitcase. My friends and I weren't really the dress-up types. "I don't think so."

"That's okay," she said kindly. "Maybe we can look through the lost and found bins at the high school after school's done for the year. There might be some stuff you can take and wear to church while you're here. Until then, you can wear something of mine."

I put my fork down, suddenly a little nauseated by the eggs and conversation. "Yeah, sure," I said, just to be nice. But I had no intention of pawing through the lost and found bins for clothes to wear to church. In my real life, I had clothes of my own, and I didn't go to church. We usually spent Sunday mornings cleaning the house, or reading in bed, or sometimes we had Amelia's gymnastics meets or my soccer practice. Just two Sundays ago, I'd played doubles tennis with Anne, Isabel, and June (we are all terrible, but it didn't matter), then we biked together to our favorite ice cream shop. I couldn't even remember the last time I'd been to church.

But here in Thistledew, I guess I was a churchgoer.

After breakfast, I called home to check on my sister. "Nothing's changed," Dad said in a whisper, explaining that Mom was asleep in the chair beside Amelia's bed. I asked if he needed to go, and he said he probably should but promised he'd call me later to get the scoop on things in Thistledew. And then we hung up. There was no mention of my drip candle, no talk of blame—but I felt sick thinking about it anyway. How long would it take for them to figure out the cause of the fire?

I stared at my cell phone for a few minutes, wondering what all my friends were up to back home. The weather was supposed to be nice there this weekend, and I knew a few of them were going into the city to go to Shedd Aquarium and out for fancy desserts somewhere. I was still in the loop enough to know what I was missing. For a second, I considered replying to one of the many texts or calls or group chats that had popped up on my screen over the past few days. But I wasn't sure I could actually talk to anyone without making myself physically ill, and how could I explain my current situation in a quick text?

Eventually, I decided to text Beckett and Anne, my two closest friends, to tell them that the cell service in Thistledew was terrible (a lie—it was surprisingly good) and that I was sorry. I *was* sorry, for so many things, but I couldn't figure out how to explain to my friends *why*. Just like I hadn't been able to talk to Doctor Bob (or Dan, or John, or whatever that hospital therapist's name was). In some ways, it was easiest not to talk to my friends at all, because then I could divide my life into there and here, then and now. I'd already decided it was going to be easiest if I just pretended my real life didn't exist, to try to make this summer something separate, even though I knew the world was moving on without me. That way I could forget about home for a few minutes at a time.

Before either of my two best friends could reply, I threw on a pair of sweats and trekked out to the backyard to check on Big Bear. He wagged his tail and bounded toward me. I was relieved to see he hadn't up and disappeared in the night. I guess part of me had expected something awful to happen—but that was the *old* part of me, the part that worried about things I couldn't control. New Maia was supposed to trust that the wandering dog would be fine; New Maia was an optimist who wasn't scared of bad things happening.

Eager to get started on my summer dog-training project, I worked with him on fetching. This was a fairly simple game where I tossed a stick and he picked it up, which seemed like a skill he'd been born with. Then I tried to teach him to sit. This was a less elegant process than the fetching. I waited until he sat down on his own, then hollered out, "Sit." Most of the time, as soon as I said the word *sit*, Bear popped right back up to standing again. I tried pushing his big fluffy butt down, while repeating "Sit . . . *sit . . . sit . . .*" over and over, but he didn't seem to understand the exercise. He was a good dog, though, and never jumped on me or barked. That felt like a win, so I gave up on *sit* for a while and decided to give him a little break for just being born good.

After I'd poured some food in Bear's bowl, I went back inside and borrowed a nice shirt from Grandma to wear to church. Luckily, all her "slacks" were too big for me, so she let me get away with wearing June's jeans. I wasn't the only one at church in jeans, but Grandma told me that wasn't the point.

Church didn't last nearly as long as I'd expected it to; we were done and on our way home before ten. Now the rest of Sunday stretched out ahead of me, with nothing on the schedule. We bumped into Griffin and a person who I assumed was his mom on our walk home after the service.

He was wearing a button-down, checkered shirt, and someone had obviously wet down his mop of hair and tried to brush it into submission. He looked miserable in his fancy church clothes, but perked up when he saw me.

"Hey, Maia!" He scampered over, tugging at his top button. "This is my mom, Wendy."

"Hi," I said, smiling my parent smile.

"She prefers to be called Wendy," Griffin declared. "Instead of missus anything, since she still has my dad's last name and she doesn't like it. Mom, this is my friend Maia, who is staying with Howard and Bea and whose house burned down." As soon as he said it, his hand flew up to cover his mouth.

Wendy looked at me with sad eyes. "Oh, hon, I'm sorry . . . Griffin shouldn't have brought it up." She put her hand on Griffin's head and steered him under her arm.

"It's okay," I said, and meant it. It was nice to get the facts out in the open and not pretend I was just here in Thistledew for a fun summer vacation or something.

Grandpa grunted, "We all know what happened, so why ignore the topic?"

I looked at him, surprised to hear the usually quiet old man say exactly what I was thinking.

Grandma artfully changed the subject. "Wendy, I was thinking about taking Maia over to the lake this afternoon, show her the beach and give her a little tour of the area. Would Griffin like to come along?"

"Please?" Griffin begged his mom. "Please, please, *please*?"

I could see Wendy sizing me up, possibly trying to decide if my family's bad luck was contagious. I'd noticed some people doing that after the fire. I bet Wendy was thinking: *If I send my son off with her, will he suffer the same awful fate her sister had under her care?* After a long moment's consideration, Griffin's mom looked at Grandma and said, "Sure. I need to clean the house this afternoon, which would be easier without my little mess maker around."

"Do *not* recycle my fort!" Griffin shouted. "It's not trash. It's my greatest treasure."

"Here's the deal: I won't touch your boxes," Wendy assured him. "If you promise to take those swimming lessons at the lake without grumbling this summer."

"No deal," Griffin muttered under his breath. "I don't swim."

"What's that?" Wendy said with a laugh, holding her hand against her ear like a funnel. "*Sure*, you say? Sounds good, Mom?"

"We can discuss this at a later date," Griffin declared.

Laughing, I decided I already loved this kid.

CHAPTER SEVEN

An hour or so later, Grandma, Griffin, and I climbed into the old Buick and headed out of town toward the community beach on the near end of Lake Vermilion. I'd glanced at the map hanging on the wall of my den and realized Lake Vermilion was huge. I'd been expecting a little pit of a lake, something small and cozy. But Vermilion dominated the landscape up here in northern Minnesota. Even so, it was nothing like Lake Michigan back home in Chicago. Lake Michigan seemed endless and looked more like an ocean with its white-capped waves and rugged wildness.

Lake Vermilion had all these little bends and twists and inlets and islands that made it feel quaint and welcoming. Not nearly as terrifying as any of the Great Lakes, but still scary to *me* because it was a lake and very deep. I never went in past my chest in lakes, and I always avoided the deep end in pools. My fear of heights kept me off diving boards, as a rule, so there had never really been a reason for me to venture into any dark, scary deep ends anyway. My sister *loved* diving boards and zip-lining into water, and she was always trying to coax me into giving it a try. "Just close your eyes and jump!" she'd say. "If I can do it, you definitely can!"

But I *couldn't* do it. Maybe someday I'd work up the nerve, but that day hadn't happened yet.

Grandma pulled her car into a spot in the near-empty lot out at the beach and then set off on her daily walk up and down the little strip of road that went along the edge of the lake, leaving me and Griffin alone to explore for a while. We sat down on the wide stretch of brown, gritty sand beside the water, and I followed Griffin's lead as he began piling small stones and sticks to make a little fortress on the beach. "My mom told me I'm not supposed to ask you any questions about your sister, so you don't have to answer this if you don't want." Griffin looked up somberly, then went back to poking a stick in the sand.

"What's your question?" I asked him. I really hoped he wasn't going to ask me if she was going to die, or if I'd started the fire, or why I hadn't put it out before it took over the house, or anything like that. I didn't like to think about my answer to those kinds of questions. I glanced at him and added, "Once I know what the question is, then I'll decide if I want to answer or not."

Griffin looked relieved. "Do you like her?"

I frowned. "What do you mean, do I like her?"

"Your sister. Is she the good kind of sister, or the kind that bugs you? Do you guys fight? How old is she?"

"First of all, she's nine." I swallowed and looked him in the eye. "Same as you. And she's the good kind of sister. The best."

Griffin nodded. I guess this was the answer he'd been hoping for. "I've always wanted a little brother. But my friends at school, some of them have big families, and they're always complaining about it. It seems like most people don't like their siblings, but I've always thought it would be great to have at least one. A built-in friend." He looked at me seriously. "What's she like?"

"Well," I said, trying to think of how to describe Amelia. "She loves making up games and stories, she loves gymnastics, she's really good at distracting people when they're worried about stuff, and she's usually funny but in the roll-your-eyes kind of way."

"What does that mean?" Griffin asked.

"Her favorite book is called *Dad Jokes*, if that tells you anything. So she's always blurting out the worst jokes ever, but they crack her up and when she laughs, it makes everyone else laugh." I took a breath, trying to think of something that would capture the essence of my sister. It was hard to summarize someone in just a few words, especially her. But then I thought of exactly what to say about her that would help someone like Griffin understand. "Also: She's convinced she's going to become a superhero when she grows up."

Griffin grinned. "The kind of superhero that develops their powers later in life or gets their powers in a lab, like Spider-Man? Or the kind of superhero that discovers they were born with a hidden superstrength and uses it for good, like Wonder Woman?"

I laughed. "I'm pretty sure she thinks she was born with a superpower and is just waiting for it to show itself. Or that she'll move somewhere new, like Superman did, and discover her hidden power."

"Cool," Griffin said definitively. He stood up and walked to the edge of the lake, dragging his bare toe through the chilly water. "I think it's neat that you're friends with your sister. All the thirteen-year-olds I know are crabby and think they're too cool to hang out with little kids. And most people I know don't like their sisters."

I snorted. "Well, I'm not technically thirteen yet, so I guess there's still a chance I'll wake up crabby on my next birthday. But I do like third graders, most of them anyway. And I definitely love my sister."

"I hope she's okay," Griffin said quietly from the edge of the lake. "I'm sorry she got hurt."

"Yeah," I said. "Me too."

"Do you want to be done talking about her now?"

"I think so," I said. "Yeah."

Griffin shifted gears quickly. While I was still busy thinking about Amelia, he raced out of the ankle-deep water, unzipped his backpack, and pulled out his Bear Scout guidebook. "Here are all the badges we need to do this summer if I'm going to finish everything: Forensics, Critter Care, A Bear Goes Fishing, Bear Picnic Basket—"

I cut him off. "Those aren't the real names. You're making that list up."

"They are!" Griffin insisted, shoving the book toward me. "It's what the badges are called."

"Why do they make them all sound so stupid?" I glanced

down the rest of the list of Bear Scout badges, reading them aloud. "Make It Move, Marble Madness, Roaring Laughter." I rolled my eyes and gave Griffin a look. "Seriously? If they have to call this one 'Roaring Laughter,' I can pretty much guarantee it's not going to be fun or funny."

Griffin's face fell. "Do you not want to help me anymore?"

"I didn't say that," I said quickly, reminding myself not to act like a crabby thirteen-year-old. "I just think these activity names are kinda . . . well, unappealing." I read the last few on the list. "Robotics sounds cool, and I'm sort of curious what this one—Salmon Run—is all about. Super Science looks promising." I pointed to the last badge on the list. "But A World of Sound? That just sounds like a bad science class or choir video." I noticed a few things on the list were crossed out. "What's the deal with Beat of the Drum and Grin and Bear It?"

"We worked on the Beat of the Drum badge together as a den," Griffin explained. "A bunch of us got to visit the Native American reservation outside town, and we met with some members of the Minnesota Chippewa Tribe. Some people from the tribe talked about how it's not right to borrow or use other people's traditions in the wrong way." He lowered his voice to a whisper. "We ended up skipping a lot of the official badge requirements, since our troop leader feels like the most important work for this badge is us learning more about Native American culture and history."

"That makes sense," I said.

"The tribe leaders invited us to watch this really amazing dance ceremony, and then they told us stories so we could understand the history of why they did the event." Griffin sighed. "It was so cool."

"So . . . you earned that badge already?" I asked, glancing at the list of requirements.

"My mom and I decided it wasn't really a badge I could ever call done," Griffin said. "It's not like you can spend a couple hours learning a few things about someone else's life and culture, and then call it good. I mean, you wouldn't want me to spend an hour talking to you and then decide that the things I learn in that hour is all there is to know about you, right?"

"Yeah," I said, nodding. "That's a very good point. I think you guys made the right call."

"At least I *started* doing work to earn that badge, right?" Griffin said. "That's better than not doing anything at all, and I'm excited to learn more."

"Okay, so what about the Grin and Bear It badge?" I asked.

"We hosted a carnival for the second-grade Wolf pack a couple weeks ago. That was fun, too, but not as interesting as visiting the reservation."

"So you have two badges you've started or finished, and a dozen or so to go?"

"Eleven," Griffin clarified, in a way that reminded me so much of my sister. "Eleven to go."

"Totally doable," I said. I scanned the requirements Griffin needed to meet to earn a few of the badges. "Some of these are going to be pretty quick and easy. But it looks like Salmon Run is a swimming badge," I said, wiggling my eyebrows. "I heard your mom say something about swimming lessons after church this morning . . . that seems like a good way for you to finish that one."

Griffin kicked at one of his sand huts, destroying the eastern edge of our land. "I hate swimming lessons," he said. "I don't like to put my face in the water."

"If it makes you feel better," I said, "neither do I. I'm scared of the deep end of the pool, and I never go out past where I can touch the bottom in lakes."

"Really?" he asked, grinning. "But you're big. You're not supposed to be scared of things."

"Ha," I sighed. "I wish fears were something you grew out of."

"Maybe you should take lessons with me this summer! If you were there, I don't think I would be as scared."

"I doubt they'd put us in the same class," I said, unwilling to admit to Griffin that swimming lessons were absolutely out of the question.

"The lessons are here at the beach, in the lake," he said. "It's all ages together. Sometimes, there are even adults in the class. My mom signed me up for the class last year, but I quit after a few weeks." He cringed. "I cried every Tuesday and Thursday afternoon, whenever it got close to swimming-lesson time. My mom let me skip a few classes, and then finally said she was tired of fighting about it, so I won that war."

"Oh," I said, smiling as the image of Griffin and his mom battling each other with plastic swords popped into my mind. Wendy seemed like the kind of mom who would be willing to play sword-battle with her kid.

"At the end of the summer lessons, they inflate this huge climbing wall thing and have a giant slide out in the water at the edge of the buoys. If they think you're a strong enough swimmer, you get to swim out to play on it." He looked out at the water wistfully. "It looks so fun, but Mom says I can't go out there—even with a life jacket on—until she feels confident that I could swim back to shore without assistance."

"The only way you're going to be a better swimmer is to take lessons," I said, feeling bad for taking Griffin's mom's side in the argument.

Griffin rolled his eyes at me. "If you're twelve or older, you get to play on all the fun bouncy stuff in the water, but also . . ." He paused dramatically. "If you get good enough, you might be allowed to swim out to the raft and jump off." Griffin pointed to a wooden raft floating way out in the middle of the bay.

The elderly floating structure looked like it was miles away; halfway to Canada, probably. I could never swim to that raft. What if I got a leg cramp halfway out and slipped under the surface and drowned? What if a fish bit my leg and I couldn't kick anymore and I drowned? What if I got out there and I got freaked out having to climb up the ladder onto the raft, and I fell back into the water, hit my head, and drowned? Every single scenario I could imagine ended with me drowning.

As those fears washed over me, I remembered my promise to myself—that this summer, I would work on being Maia the Brave. Maia Who Does Things. Maia Who Isn't Scared All the Time. I thought about how surprised my family and friends would be if they heard I'd started swimming in a lake. How excited and proud Amelia would be to hear I could swim way out in a sea of deep, dark water. If I took swimming lessons with Griffin and got brave enough to swim in deep water, helping my friend stay safe, that would be a way to prove to myself—and my family—that I'd changed. That I was New Maia: strong, brave, and capable.

But most important, Griffin needed me. If I joined the lessons, I would be helping him go for it, too. "I'll do it," I told him, before I talked myself back out of it. "You're gonna earn all eleven of your badges this summer, *and* we're gonna get good enough to swim out to that inflatable slide in the water. But the deal is, we have to help each other, so neither one of us will give up, okay? That means I help you out with your Bear badges, and you promise to take swimming lessons with me, no whining or crying or fighting with your mom. Deal?"

Griffin looked out at the lake, then down at his Bear Scout book. Finally, he nodded and held out his small hand to shake mine. "Lady, we've got a deal."

CHAPTER EIGHT

"Kid." I woke early Monday morning to find Grandpa Howard standing in my bedroom doorway, silhouetted by light from the kitchen. "Get dressed and get a move on." It was still dark outside, even darker in my room. And Grandpa was barking orders that I wasn't ready to follow at this time of day.

"So early?" I groaned. I glanced at the clock—6:04. I never even got up this early on school days. Technically, this was summer break, which was supposed to mean leisurely mornings. Griffin was at school, Grandma had to work at the Y Store today, and I had a whole day—the whole summer, really—stretching out empty before me. "What's the rush, Pops?"

"I'm ready to go," he said.

This didn't answer the question of why *I* had to get up at the crack of dawn. I pulled my blanket and sheet over my head and hoped he'd forget I was there.

"Be outside in ten minutes," he said. "Bea left a muffin and some fruit in a bag on the counter for you. You can take it with you and eat it later."

As soon as he'd closed the den door behind him, I groaned into my pillow and reluctantly rolled out of bed. I pulled on a pair of sweats and a T-shirt with Anne's hockey team logo on it and shuffled into the bathroom to brush my teeth in a daze.

There was a soft canvas lunch sack sitting on the kitchen table—I assumed this was for me. I peeked inside and saw the promised muffin (freshly baked!) and a container of fruit. There was also a juice box, the kind I used to get in my lunch in elementary school. I smiled, grabbed the bag, and headed out the door.

Outside, Bear greeted me with a head bump against my thigh and a small moan. "Hey, big guy," I said. "You're up early, too, huh?"

"When you finish chatting with the wildlife, I'd love to get going." Grandpa was sitting astride his motorcycle, helmet on, bug screen flipped up. There was a second helmet resting on the back of the bike.

"That helmet doesn't look like it will fit Bear, Pops," I said, giving Grandpa a wary look. "I'd guess he's more of an extra large."

"Very funny," Grandpa Howard said in a humorless tone, gesturing to the helmet. "Put it on and hop up."

"Nope."

"Nope?"

"I told you, I don't do motorcycles. They're death vehicles."

I was pretty sure I caught a hint of a smile play at the corners of Grandpa's mouth, but he swallowed it down before it became the full deal. "I've been driving this cycle for fifty years," he sighed. "I wouldn't let you on it if I didn't know it was safe."

I crossed my arms. "You've been driving this thing for

fifty years? Even more reason to not get on the deathmobile. Shouldn't it be condemned or rotted out by now?"

Grandpa coughed, and I think it might have been to hide a laugh. I lifted an eyebrow to show him I'd noticed. "Not this *exact* motorcycle," he clarified. "There have been a few different ones over the years. But this one's my favorite."

"Why?" I asked. "Because it's the only one that isn't a crushed heap of metal on the side of the highway?"

"Because it fits two riders. Which means I get to take a friend along, and this summer, that friend is you." Grandpa fixed me with a firm stare. "Now, come on. We've got work to do." He turned the key and revved the motor. Bear skulked away, probably heading toward his little hut in the backyard for another hour or three of sleep. Smart dog.

I closed my eyes, crossed my fingers, and hoped the prayers I'd said at yesterday morning's church service would protect me today from certain doom. "New Maia," I muttered through clenched teeth. Then I tossed my sack of breakfast in the little storage box on the back of the motorcycle and climbed aboard.

The first few seconds on the back of the cycle felt very strange, especially since Grandpa was driving slow and it felt more like we were riding on a noisy tandem bike that no one had to pedal. I kept my eyes closed while we breezed by Griffin and Wendy's house. When we turned onto Main Street, the cycle leaned dangerously far to one side and I eked out a little scream inside my helmet. We were halfway through town before it stopped feeling weird to wrap my arms tight around my grandpa's soft wool jacket. He turned on some country music and cranked it up just loud enough that we could both hear it through our helmets and over the sound of the wind.

By the time we shot out the other end of town, my eyes were wide open. I'd begun to appreciate the cool feeling of fresh morning air whipping against my hands. My sweatpants were fluttering in the wind, pressed tight against my knees. But I was shielded from most of the wind by Grandpa Howard's firm back, and I began to relax and enjoy the ride. I still didn't know where we were going, but I was curious to find out and happy to be invited along on Grandpa's adventure.

As Grandpa drove down the desolate highway, I watched the trees and signs blur into a foggy comet of colors as we buzzed past. There was a tiny old airplane propped up in someone's front yard outside town, with a big FOR SALE sign hanging from its propeller. We passed a Smokey Bear sign— "Fire Bear," as Amelia had always called him—holding a sign that said: ONLY YOU CAN PREVENT FOREST FIRES! Under that was a changeable sign that said: FIRE DANGER: MEDIUM. The forest was thick on either side of us, but at one point I caught sight of a pair of deer leaping through the undergrowth, their puffy white tails flickering like little beacons amid all that green.

Just a few miles outside town, Grandpa slowed down and pulled over to the side of the highway. The motorcycle's tires popped and crackled over the loose stones on the side of the road. Suddenly, we veered right, onto a small gravel road that I probably wouldn't have noticed was even there if we'd been driving by in a car. Tree branches hung low overhead, and the road was narrow—it would be tight to fit a car down this lane without scratching up the sides. But Grandpa and I rolled smoothly down the center of the road, trees stretching toward us from either side. The motorcycle bumped and bounced over the rough surface, but I'd already gotten used to the loose feeling of riding on the back of the cycle.

About a half mile down this hidden road, we came to a dead end. The road just stopped. Grandpa turned off the ignition, we both pulled off our helmets, and the sounds of the forest came alive around us: wind whistling through the trees, birdcalls in surround sound, the crunch of Grandpa's boot against the loose rocks underfoot.

"Where are we?" I asked, grabbing my bagged breakfast out of the storage box. I reached into the sack and pulled off the muffin top, delighted to find it was still just a tad warm from Grandma's oven.

Grandpa set off up a narrow trail that led sharply uphill. He turned back. "I'll show you."

I shrugged and followed. It felt good to stretch my legs, and I liked to think the clean forest air was a salve for my damaged lungs. My toe—still taped to its neighbor—wasn't throbbing anymore, so I had no trouble keeping up with Grandpa's brisk pace. As we walked up the trail, I tried to take in my surroundings. But I was soon huffing and puffing, and I found if I didn't stare straight down at my own two feet, I kept tripping on rocks and roots that were sticking out of the ground at odd angles. So it came as a complete surprise when suddenly we emerged from the forested trail and stepped onto a huge mass of rock at the top of a clearing.

And then I noticed the tower.

Straight ahead of me was a tall mass of steel and iron, stretching up into the sky, high above the world. I recognized it at once—this was the fire tower, the one Grandma had pointed out on the way into town Saturday afternoon. I shuddered as I noticed the endless set of stairs that led up, up, up to a looming platform a million miles above us.

"Come on up," Grandpa said, breaking the silence. He stepped onto the bottom stair of the tower and began to climb. "I'll show you around."

I pointed at a sign hanging askew at the top of the first set of metal stairs. "It says 'No Trespassing. By order of the Forest Service.' That sounds official."

"I *am* the Forest Service," Grandpa said, then added, "Retired Forest Service. This is my tower."

"Are you telling me you own this tower?" I asked, skeptical.

"The government owns the tower. But I've been keeping watch up here for years. They assigned me to fire watch duty back when I first joined the Forest Service, and then I picked it back up again after I retired." Grandpa had just said more words in a row than I think I'd ever heard come out of his mouth before. And none of them made much sense.

"So you . . . sit up there and watch for fires in the forest?" I asked.

"Yes."

"Don't they have drones or something to do that?"

"There are planes that scan the area," Grandpa said, sounding a little agitated. "But no fancy technology will ever be better than a human eye."

I cocked my head. "No offense, but I'd argue that a plane can probably cover more ground than your view from this tower." I grinned at him.

He did not smile back.

"Do they pay you to sit up there and watch for fires?" I asked, craning my neck to try to figure out exactly how far one could see out the top of the tower. "How often do you do this? Have you ever actually spotted any flames?" Suddenly, I felt nervous—what if there _were_ a fire, and we were trapped way out here in the middle of a giant woodpile? We were several miles up a hill, in a wood-filled forest that could easily go up in flames at any second.

"I come out here every day," Grandpa said, answering only one of my questions. I wasn't sure I wanted to know the answer to the third thing I'd asked.

"Every day?" That seemed a little extreme, but I wasn't going to say it aloud.

"Forest fires don't take weekends off." Grandpa set off up the stairs again, bounding up two at a time like a man half his age. "Your grandmother doesn't like the idea of leaving you home alone at the house, so whenever she's working, you're going to come out here with me. So, you may as well get used to it. You'll like the view. Come on up."

"I can't," I said. Just looking at the stairs was making me feel nauseous. "I'm afraid of heights."

Grandpa gave me a look that told me he didn't approve. Pops was the kind of guy who seemed like he'd never been afraid of anything. But even his disapproving look wasn't going to change my mind. This was too much. How could I be expected to climb up a rickety, falling apart tower and actually *search* for fire, when all I wanted was to never see or hear a fire of any kind again?

"Yeah, no," I said, more to myself than to him. "Not happening."

"Suit yourself," he said. Then he turned and headed up the tower stairs, leaving me alone—in the middle of a giant rock on top of a hill, lost deep in the woods, wanting nothing more than to be able to climb up that tower after him, just so I didn't have to be alone with my own fears.

CHAPTER NINE

The rest of the week dragged in slow motion, each day feeling like a repeat of the one before it.

Every morning, Grandpa and I got up early and set off into the woods to his fire tower post. He'd climb up the stairs and do whatever it was he did at the top all day, while I sat at the base of the fire tower and read or knit (Grandma was teaching me how) or listened to music. Sometimes, when I got bored, I'd try to climb up a few steps, just to see if I could. I'll admit, I was a little curious about what was up at the top of the tower. But as soon as I was a few feet above solid ground, my breath would quicken and my chest would get tight and I'd feel like puking. So then I'd back down the three or four steps I had climbed up so fast that I almost always stumbled before I even reached the bottom.

Sometime before noon, Grandpa would come down to pee in the woods, and then we'd sit together on a rock overlooking the valley below and eat a sandwich or pasta salad that Grandma had packed up for us that morning before leaving for work at the Y Store.

Every afternoon once we got back to town, Bear and I would sit out front and wait for Griffin's bus to pull up at the end of Grandma and Grandpa's dead-end road. As soon as I saw his little mop of hair bopping off the bus, I'd open my book and pretend I hadn't been eagerly awaiting his return, like a dog staring out the window waiting for its human to get home from work.

Before dinner, Griffin and I would work on different stuff he needed to do to earn one of his Cub Scout badges, and this single hour of actual human interaction each day was my only salvation. The two of us spent most afternoons that first week in Thistledew researching and building different musical instruments, which was super fun. One afternoon we made a rain stick out of paper towel tubes and dry grains of rice. Another day, we used tools and scraps of wood and metal we found in my grandparents' shed to make an amateur version of an instrument called a mbira. This was a little thumb-piano-type thing that was developed by the Shona people from Zimbabwe, and Griffin and I decided I should take it home to my sister. She'd love it.

Every night after dinner, I'd FaceTime with my parents. They looked awful. Even though they wouldn't ever turn their phone screens to give me a glimpse of Amelia's bed, I knew from what I'd been told that she looked awful, too. She was still sedated and her skin wrapped, which doctors said was important to her recovery. Her leg—one of the few parts of her body that hadn't been burned—was wrapped in a stiff cast. Since she had so much healing to do, my parents kept assuring me that it was in everyone's best interest that I was gone for the summer. They spent all their spare time at the hospital and trying to deal with insurance stuff and figuring out what to do about our house.

No one had said anything yet about the cause of the fire, and I hadn't brought it up. I guess the arson investigator was swamped and backlogged, and since the back half of our house had been almost totally destroyed, it was going to take time for them to sort through everything. Mom didn't like to talk about that night at all, since I guess she blamed herself for the fact that the fire alarm by the bedroom wasn't working. She'd been the one dealing with the construction guys on a day-to-day basis, she pointed out, and she knew they'd been fiddling with the wiring that connected to some stuff—like our smoke detectors—upstairs. She hadn't checked to make sure the batteries were fresh, and that guilt was eating her up. Dad argued it was *his* fault, since he was the one who pushed so hard for a new electrical panel as part of the project.

I knew exactly how Mom and Dad felt, and wished I could erase their guilt by admitting it was my candle that had actually *started* the fire. That meant *I* was the one responsible for almost killing my sister, destroying my home, and saddling my parents with guilt they shouldn't have been carrying. Everyone kept trying to convince me I was some kind of hero for dashing through the flames to pull Amelia out of the fire, but I *wasn't* a hero—I was more like a villain with a conscience. If she'd died in that fire, I would have been a murderer. Eventually, we'd probably have to talk about what I'd done and how I'd ruined all our lives, but that time hadn't come yet. If they knew, I might never get to come home.

In every phone conversation, I asked my parents when I might get to come back, but they both kept making up reasons not to hear me or answer. Instead, Dad went overboard assuring me that my sister was fine with me not being there. Even though she was usually pretty out of it, they let me read a few chapters from *The One and Only Ivan* aloud over the phone each night. She and I had already read the book together last year, so it didn't matter if she could follow along or not—but I hoped she could. Even though it was a sometimes-sad book, I knew Ivan and Stella and Bob would be the perfect escape from her pain and that horrible hospital.

Each day, during lunch on our rock, I asked Grandpa some questions about the fire tower. I learned that he'd been keeping watch—off and on—in this tower since he was a teenager. He liked the solitude, I guess. I couldn't tell if he was actually getting paid to do this job, or if it was some sort of volunteer thing. He was a little cagey with details about almost everything.

"So, have you ever actually *seen* a fire from up there?" I asked on Thursday, over a picnic lunch of cheese, crackers, and grapes. Even Grandpa got a Capri Sun to drink that day, which I found pretty funny—especially when I had to poke the straw into the foil pouch for him.

"Of course," he said, munching on a cracker. "Plenty of times. If I hadn't, you think I'd bother sitting up here?"

"So, what happens when you see something?" I asked.

Grandpa took a deep breath. "Well, first I eyeball where

the fire is, then I use a special tool to get a more accurate reading of exactly where the smoke is. Then I radio it in, and someone from the office heads out and checks things out. Lots of times, it's just someone who's started a brush fire and let it burn a little too big. Sometimes, it will be a small fire caused by lightning or someone's campfire getting out of control. Usually, we get those settled before they become too big of a problem. A few times, though, they get out of control quickly, and that's when spotting it early is important." He bent his head to one side and said, "If you came up in the tower, I could show you how the maps and tools work."

"Not gonna happen," I said. After a long silence, I added, "Just so you know, I have *tried* to come up. The farthest I've made it is the sixth step. Then I can't breathe and my body totally freezes up, so I crawl back to solid ground again."

"You've got a real phobia, huh?" Grandpa asked, standing up to brush a snowfall of cracker crumbs off his lap.

"I know you think it's all in my head," I muttered. I'd heard people tell me this plenty—that my fears were in my mind, and if I just pushed past them, I'd see there was nothing to worry about. I had tried to push past them plenty, but most of my fears were too huge to just shove off to the side. That's not how it worked. It's like when someone says it's best to just ignore bullies, and they'll eventually get tired of picking on you. But if a bully is sitting on your chest, pounding you in the stomach, they can be hard to just ignore.

"I have tried to *stop* being afraid of heights, lots of times, but that's not how a phobia works."

Grandpa nodded. "I know that."

"You do?"

He didn't expand, but knowing he understood—at least somewhat—made me feel better. Less ashamed. Grandpa packed up the empty containers into his backpack and took a final slurp of juice out of the silver pouch. "What do you do down here all day by yourself?"

We'd been coming out here for four days, and this was the first time he'd asked me this. "Read," I said. "Knit sometimes. Draw stuff in the gravel. Look for trash. There's a lot of it up here, you know? I think teenagers have parties here sometimes. I've found a lot of broken glass."

"You could explore, you know. Wander around in the woods."

I shook my head, having already considered this myself. "I'd probably get lost. And I'm afraid of bears."

Grandpa gave me a funny look, then began to walk away, back toward the stairs and up to his tower.

"You know what would help?" I called out after him. "If we could bring Big Bear out here, I could work on his training during the day. And if he were here to keep me company, I'd feel better about wandering around. Bear seems like the kind of dog who could help me find my way back if I got lost."

"You're not gonna get lost," Grandpa said.

"But if I *did* . . ." I said.

He shook his head and frowned, then began the slow climb up to the top of the tower.

In the moment, I didn't know what that headshake meant. But the next morning when I dragged myself out of the house to get on the back of Grandpa's motorcycle, there was Bear: sitting inside a little motorcycle sidecar, all strapped in like a regular old passenger. "Pops!" I exclaimed. Bear wagged at me, obviously proud to be part of the action. "Where did you get that?"

"Used to have a dog," he said simply. "Had this thing sitting in the back of the shed. Figure I might as well get some use out of it."

"Well, okay, then," I said, trying to act like this wasn't a big deal. But it was a *huge* deal—now I'd have someone to keep me company during the day, which would change everything!

I hopped on the back of the cycle and patted Bear's shaggy fur. "I think Grandpa's falling in love with you," I told the big dog, smiling as I settled my helmet on my head.

"Don't get any big ideas," Grandpa grunted. "I'm only bringing him along 'cause you asked me to."

I laughed, then whispered to Bear, "I guess he loves both of us."

Bear was a natural on the motorcycle. He sat nice and calm, letting his tongue hang out and blinking his eyes in the whipping wind as we rode out to the fire tower. When we got to our parking spot and started walking up the trail, Bear stayed between me and Grandpa—obviously a little apprehensive about his new turf. This told me he'd already begun to think of Grandpa and Grandma's house as home, since he looked like he felt a bit out of place here in the wild.

When we got to the trail's end, Grandpa immediately set off up the stairs. Big Bear began to climb up after him, but Grandpa shooed him away. "Get," he said, waving his hand at the dog. "Go on."

Bear stopped on the first landing, staring after Grandpa but not climbing any higher.

I called out, "See how nicely he listens to you? I think we can all agree that he's the perfect pet."

Grandpa did not respond. But I knew he must have had a soft spot for the scruffy guy, since he'd rigged up a whole sidecar on his beloved motorcycle just so we could take a dog on this adventure with us.

For a long time, Bear sat still as a statue on that first landing of the tower steps, keeping one eye trained on the stairs where Grandpa had disappeared, while also tracking my movements down below. I wasn't hard to keep tabs on; I didn't roam very far. I finally coaxed him down by offering to share part of my peanut butter sandwich (that day's breakfast). After breakfast, we both lay down on the rock—already nice and toasty from the early-morning sun that beat down on the top of the hill—and dozed for a while. Knowing I wasn't alone, vulnerable to surprise animal attacks or other terrifying scenarios, I felt comfortable sleeping on the job for the first time all week. There really wasn't anything better than a nap in the sunshine at the butt crack of dawn.

When I woke up, I lay there with my eyes open, gazing up into the blue early-morning sky. Up here, the trees made a sort of whistling sound, since many of them hadn't yet gotten their summer leaves and the branches whipped and swayed nakedly in the breeze. The sky was dotted with sparse puffs of clouds at the very edges. It hadn't rained since I'd arrived in Minnesota, and it didn't look like it was going to anytime soon. The weather was perfect.

This summer was already so different from usual. No camps, no soccer games, no sleepovers, no pool. No last-day-of-school cookout at the park, no guys versus girls Super Soaker war, no hammocking. I knew from their texts (most of which still went unanswered) that all my friends' lives were moving on as usual, but in a matter of just a few weeks, I'd popped right out of mine and gotten tossed into an alternate universe. I missed my life in Chicago, but I also didn't. I missed my friends, but I also didn't.

I missed Amelia, and there were no days I didn't.

I tried to feel grateful that at least I wasn't constantly surrounded by all the things that were suddenly missing from my life.

Once I mustered the energy to sit up again, Bear and I worked on a few basic commands—sit, lie down, and the all-too-important high-five (just for funsies). Griffin had found a book at his school library about dog training, and he'd checked it out for me during his class's weekly media center visit. I'd quickly read the whole guide cover to cover, making notes of all the most important stuff. Griffin was excited when I returned it to him a few days later—because he would get to trade it in at the library for a Dog Man book instead.

After a while, I could tell Bear was tired of work. He stopped paying attention to my commands and wandered off to the edge of the flat rock to take a pee. Then he began sniffing at the ferns and shrubs and rubble that surrounded the tower. A little while later, I cracked up when he trotted back to the spot where he'd gone to the bathroom just a few minutes before and sniffed his own marking like it was a mysterious treasure. In time, he grew more curious and explored a little farther into the forest surrounding the tower. He scared a squirrel up a tree, then barked once to tell the squirrel he was waiting until it came down again—to either eat it or to play, I wasn't sure which. I followed him, suddenly worried he'd get distracted by some sort of creature in the woods and run off. I wanted to stay close, to remind him we were out here together, and that he shouldn't go too far.

Soon, I realized I'd ventured farther off the rock than I had before. I could still easily see the tower in the distance, which gave me some comfort, so I let Bear lead me farther into the trees. We found a cluster of moss-covered boulders that looked like a gnome village. A little farther along, there were two separate trees that somehow shared one trunk—it was almost like the tree had some sort of fight with itself when it was a kid and decided to grow off in separate directions. I found a really cool flat rock that was streaked with black, amber, and maroon stripes—I put it in my pocket to give to my sister, but also planned to show Griffin, too, since he loved fun treasures.

Bear peed every twenty feet or so (usually he could only squeeze out a tiny drop), which must have been his way of marking our path so we could find the way back again. It worked. When I started getting hungry for lunch and turned to head back in the opposite direction, Bear bounded ahead of me and led me right to the bald-faced rock. Grandpa was waiting for us at the bottom of the stairs.

"Sorry!" I called out breathlessly.

"For what?"

"Disappearing like that," I said. "We were just looking around in the woods a little bit."

"Don't bother me," Grandpa said, pulling out our lunch sack. "You go where you want to go. I trust you'll find your way back."

"You do?" I asked.

"Sure," he said. "Don't you?"

I considered this. *If Grandpa trusts me to take care of myself out there, can I trust myself?* "Yeah," I said with a smile. "I guess I do."

CHAPTER TEN

With the weekend came a welcome break from fire tower duty. Though Grandpa kept up his daily ritual of trekking out to the tower, Bear and I got a few days off, since Grandma wasn't on the schedule to work at the Y Store that weekend. For the two days we'd get to spend together, Grandma Bea had planned all kinds of activities to keep me busy and make up for the time we didn't have together while she was at work.

On Saturday morning we visited one of her friends and helped sort books for the used book sale coming up at the public library a few towns over (poor Thistledew had neither a library nor a school of its own, so people had to travel a few dozen miles for both books and education). Grandma's friend Joe had set out thick slabs of coffee cake for us as a show of appreciation, and he kept refilling my lemonade cup.

Saturday afternoon, Grandma took me, Griffin, and Bear out fishing on Lake Vermilion, teaching us all kinds of stuff about different fish and fishing skills, in order to help Griffin knock off all the requirements for his A Bear Goes Fishing badge. She brought a big baggie full of candy along in the boat, and also packed up a little cooler with cold Cokes and root beer. I'd always thought fishing would be really boring. But with the never-ending candy and drinks and songs we sang that afternoon, I had a blast. The only dark spot was that Bear kept licking up all the fishy water in the bottom of the boat, which made his breath smell like death—and he was a big kisser.

That night, Wendy invited me over to eat pizza and watch a movie with her and Griffin. It was super fun, until I checked the time halfway through the movie and realized I'd missed my scheduled daily FaceTime call with my family.

"Why didn't you tell me it was so late?" I blurted out, scrambling off the couch.

Wendy yawned and wrapped her arm around Griffin. "I'm sorry, hon, I didn't realize you had to get back."

I glared at Griffin as I gathered up my stuff and shoved my feet into my shoes. He'd heard me talk about my evening check-in with my family plenty of times. He knew I couldn't miss it; that these calls were my only chance to connect with my own parents and my sister and feel like I still had *something* left from my real life anymore. I could feel hot, guilty tears springing into my eyes, but I wasn't going to let them fall. I was too mad.

Griffin settled deeper into his mom's side. "Sorry, Maia. I forgot. Maybe you can try to call them now?"

"It's too late," I snapped. "Visiting hours are over, so they're not at the hospital anymore." I hated them both in that moment. Griffin and Wendy didn't understand what it was like to not have someone to cuddle with. To not have your family beside you when you were having a bad day. They didn't know what it was like to ruin your whole family's life, and then let them down again because you were too busy having fun. "I missed my chance, and it's because I was here, and now my sister won't get to hear my voice today because I was with you."

Wendy started to stand up, to say something, but I didn't want to hear it. I had to go, had to get out of there. I'd been so wrapped up in my own life and fun that I'd let my sister down. Again.

Feeling nauseous, I raced back to Grandma and Grandpa's house and tried to FaceTime my parents, but no one answered the call. I spent the rest of the night lying in the dark in my borrowed den bedroom, weighed down by my guilt, the murky dark, and the suffocating silence, reminding myself that I was the worst sister of all time.

On Sunday, I stayed in bed until Grandma came in to check on me. "You alive in here?" she asked, pulling the curtains back.

I hissed, like a vampire would when hit with the cold, cruel light of day.

Grandma laughed, even though I wasn't actually trying to be funny. "What do you most want to do today?" she asked, settling down on the corner of my pull-out bed.

"Sleep," I whispered.

"Not an option. Try again. I won't make you go to church unless you want to, so it's your pick—anything you want. Canoeing, hiking, go to the wolf center, go swimming, hit the library . . ." She trailed off.

What did I most want to do? I closed my eyes and

considered this. I knew Grandma wanted me to pick something from her list of options, but if she wanted the truth, here it was: "I want to go home. I want to see my sister."

Grandma's face crumpled. "Oh, hon. I know you do."

I began to cry.

"I thought we were keeping you plenty busy," she said, sounding sort of desperate. "Giving you fun things to do to keep your mind off things back in Chicago."

I let a sob slip out and hiccuped. "You are. It's just that I miss her and when you asked me what I want to do, you said that I can pick anything, and that's what I want."

"I'm afraid that's not an option," Grandma said. She looked sad to have to say it, but I could also tell from the look on her face that there wasn't any changing her mind. This whole summer had been decided without me, and I was at the mercy of my own terrible failures and the awful night that destroyed all our lives.

Grandma sat there as I cried, rubbing my foot through the blankets. After a while, she said, "Get it all out, okay?" She didn't seem to realize that no matter how hard or how long I cried, I'd *never* get it all out. "When you're ready, I'll make you some breakfast and we can come up with the plan for the day. Do you like pancakes?"

"Yes," I whimpered. "I love pancakes."

"With chocolate chips or blueberries?" She smiled at me, and I could tell she was grateful I had answered the question.

"Blueberries, please."

"Of course," she said, patting my foot again. Then she stood up, brushed at the front of her pants to get the wrinkles out, and returned to the kitchen.

I lay there, trying to calm myself. Eventually, I headed to the bathroom and washed my face. When I came out, I reminded myself that I was trying to be strong—for my parents, who wanted me gone right now; for my grandparents, who were trying to make all of this easier for me; for my sister, who hadn't asked for any of this to happen; and for me, because I wasn't willing to feel this way for the rest of my life.

· · ·

Because of all the promises I'd made to myself—and to Griffin—over the past week, I actually managed to muster up the nerve to show up at our first swim class the following Tuesday evening. The sun now set late enough each day that they could hold the class in the after-dinner hours. With all the unseasonably warm and dry spring weather, the lake water wasn't as cold as usual. So they were able to start lessons before school had even let out for summer.

Everyone kept saying the lake's temperature was unusually warm for this time of year, but I didn't have any way to know what was normal and what wasn't. The idea of swim lessons in a *lake* seemed bizarre to me, in general, but I guess that's how things work in a town without a pool. Also, the lessons were free. That seemed totally crazy, too, coming from a city where almost everything cost a fortune.

Griffin and I were going to ride out to the lake together in his mom's car. It was the first time I'd seen either of them since I'd blown up and blamed them for my own mistake that weekend.

"I'm sorry I was rude to you the other night," I said as we loaded into the car. Wendy had been friendly enough when I met them at their house, but Griffin was much quieter than usual as we each climbed into the back seat.

"It's okay," Wendy assured me, flashing me a quick smile in the rearview mirror.

"It's not," I said. "It wasn't either of your fault, and I shouldn't have freaked out like that." I took a deep breath. It felt better to get it off my chest, even if it was embarrassing to admit I'd overreacted. "I was just upset and I kind of took it out on you guys."

Griffin still didn't say anything. He was wearing a cute little life jacket over his swim trunks and rash guard. He refused to take the jacket off, even for the car ride. He just strapped his seat belt right over the puffy life jacket and crossed his arms over his chest. "They can't make me take this off," he blurted out to no one in particular a few minutes into the ride to the beach.

Wendy and I exchanged a smile. "No one's going to make you take off your life jacket during the first lesson, little duck," Wendy assured him.

"I won't, even if they tell me I have to," Griffin insisted.

"Fair enough," his mom said.

"But don't worry, because I'll be right there next to you if you need me," I promised.

I guess this was enough to crack him. Griffin reached across the back seat and took my hand. I suppose this was his way of saying he forgave me. In that moment, he reminded me so much of my sister that it ached. I wonder if he realized I needed him just as much as he needed me. I looked over and smiled. He squeezed my hand in response.

When we got to the beach, there were already a few other people gathered near the lifeguard chair. A couple of chatty older men told me they had signed up for lessons, hoping to improve their water confidence enough that they could start swimming laps around the buoys in the summertime. There were also two kids—both girls—who looked like they were in fourth or fifth grade, a lady who was somewhere between college and parent years, and a sullen-looking boy who was probably about my age. The most entertaining person there was a four or five-year-old who kept escaping his dad's arms and making a run for the water.

There were three teachers who would be leading the lessons—one was a really cute teenage boy, who I hoped was assigned to my group. There was also a stern-looking middle-aged lady teacher, and a big guy with a beard that looked like a giant bird's nest.

We all introduced ourselves, talked about our swimming experience and goals, and then they broke us into groups according to level and introduced us to our teachers. My group got the bearded guy, whose name was Evan. There were only four of us who would be working with Evan: me,

Griffin, and the two girls I'd guessed were in fourth or fifth grade. It turned out they were twins named Ellen and Hannah, they were living at a summer home on the lake with their mom for the summer, and they didn't like to talk to anyone except each other.

"Summer people," Griffin explained in a whisper. "They're all weird and unfriendly. Think they're better than the locals."

I gave him a look. "*I'm* a summer person," I reminded him.

Griffin giggled. "You're different." I decided this was a pretty sweet compliment.

At first, I was embarrassed that I'd been put into the little-kid group (except the runaway five-year-old, who was alone with the scary teacher), but I guess it made sense. I had been honest about my previous swimming experience: I'd had some lessons, but I didn't like to get my head wet and I refused to swim in water that went up past my chest.

Evan decided to start our first group lesson by putting us all in life jackets and letting us bob around to get comfortable just *being* in the water. At first, everything was going well—I borrowed a life jacket from the lifeguard tower, slipped it on, and started joking around with Griffin as we waded into the water.

But then, suddenly, I smelled smoke. We weren't in Grandpa's yard—this smoke didn't belong here. The smell of it, that feeling of something *not right*, flipped a panic switch in my head. My breath quickened. My heart started to race. I couldn't move.

"Maia?" Griffin said, tugging on my hand. "You okay?"

All of a sudden, Evan barked out, "Hey! You gotta put that out!" Something about my swim teacher's sharp, powerful shout kicked me from panic to full-blown terror. I spun in circles in ankle-deep water, searching for the fire. There, all the way across the beach, a group of teenagers had lit a small bonfire. It crackled and popped in the warm evening air, sending sparks of orange embers and curls of smoke up over the water. As soon as I saw the flames, the feeling of being trapped took over. I was frozen in the water, locked inside the tight clutches of my life jacket, transported back to that night.

The hot, acrid smell and the hazy chokehold of the fire.

My sister screaming.

The flames eating at her body.

Me pulling, tugging, always just a step behind.

I didn't realize I was screaming and crying until Wendy had me in her arms. She'd run across the beach, her eyes wide and confused. "It's okay," she said into my ear, clutching me close while trying to pull off my life jacket. "It's okay." It took everything in me not to throw up.

Meanwhile, Evan had hustled over to the group of teens and dumped a bucket of water on their fire to put it out. From somewhere far, far away, I could hear him telling the kids that fires weren't permitted anywhere on the beach, and that they could only be started in designated firepits.

Closer in, I could hear Wendy shushing me, and Griffin asking her if I was going to be okay.

I waited to see what Wendy would say, but she didn't answer. Because no one knew the answer to that question, not even me.

Would I be okay?

Would Amelia be okay?

Would my family be okay?

"She'll be fine," his mom said finally. I closed my eyes and rocked in Wendy's arms, wishing so much that it was my own mom's or dad's arms around me. Squeezing my shoulder, Wendy said, "Let's get you both home."

CHAPTER ELEVEN

That night, the nightmares began. Ever since the fire, I hadn't been dreaming—at least, not that I could remember when I woke in the morning. But that night, after my first failed swim lesson, I dreamed about the accident.

In my dream, Amelia was trapped behind a glass wall and I could see the flames inching closer and closer to her, but I couldn't break through. I woke up before I ever managed to reach her and was afraid to fall back asleep in case the dream started up again. I hated to think about how it might end.

The next morning, it was almost impossible to drag myself out of bed for fire tower duty. I could see the dream replaying in my mind, over and over. My head felt fuzzy and my body weak from too little sleep. Grandpa Howard didn't ask how I was feeling, and I didn't say anything about the dream. He wasn't a sharing kind of guy.

On the drive out to the tower, I wrapped my fingers tight in Bear's fur and tried to stop seeing my sister, sucked deeper and deeper into the flames. But no matter what I did, I couldn't unsee it, even when I squeezed my eyes tight until the space behind my eyelids went black with streaks of white.

When we got out to our usual parking spot tucked deep in the woods, I couldn't handle the thought of spending the day alone with no one other than Bear to talk to. So I decided I'd try to get Grandpa talking, to see if I could delay my alone time. "Hey, Pops?" I said as we neared the top of the trail.

He grunted in response. Not a great start.

"Are you the only one who ever works in this tower?"

"Yup."

"Have you had any other jobs?"

"Yup."

"What was your favorite?" I asked. When this question was met with complete silence, I added, "I mean, you can pick the job that was the most exciting, or the one with the best coworkers, or the one where you got good snacks . . ." I trailed off. Okay, so maybe he didn't like to talk about himself. I knew he wasn't a big fan of questions, but I just couldn't bear the thought of being alone today. I had to do *something* to try to keep him from climbing those stairs. Finally, I blurted out, "Do you need to go up the tower today?"

There was a long pause while I waited, again, for him to respond. When he didn't, I added, "I was just thinking, maybe we could hike around in the woods together instead?"

"Can't," he said finally.

"Can't?" I asked. "Or don't want to?"

"Both," he said. By this point, we had reached the crest of the big hill and I could see the stairs up to the tower looming ahead of us.

Since simple trickery didn't seem to be working, I decided

to try appealing to his sensitive side. "So, the thing is," I began. "I had a really bad dream last night, about the fire and Amelia after I sort of panicked at my swim lesson yesterday. I guess I just really don't want to be alone down here all day."

"You've got the dog," he pointed out.

"I know," I said. "And that helps. I mean, don't get me wrong, I really appreciate that he's out here and everything. It's just, I kind of want someone to talk to who might talk back." In fairness, Grandpa didn't say much more than Bear did, but at least there was always the *potential* for conversation.

"Then climb the stairs," he said.

I looked at him, wondering if he'd forgotten the reason I had been sitting by myself on a rock all day every day instead of climbing up with him for a peek at the view. "I can't," I reminded him.

"You haven't even tried," he argued.

"I have," I said, my voice now just a squeak. "Remember? Last week, I tried climbing up partway, but I never even got to the first landing."

"So you tried once," he said bluntly. "Try again."

Right then, I realized Grandpa scared me. And if I was being totally honest, I wasn't entirely sure I actually liked him all that much. After coming out here to spend time together every day for the past week and a half, I still felt like we knew almost nothing about each other. But even worse, he wasn't friendly and didn't seem to care much about anyone other than himself.

Maybe he was the reason why we hardly ever came here to visit Mom's hometown and family. Because her dad's a grump and it's totally possible he never *wanted* us to come. I mean, he spent every night out in an old camper in the backyard all alone, he wouldn't let a sweet stray dog come in the house for shelter, and he hadn't asked me anything about my sister since I'd arrived. The only reason he took me out here with him every morning was because Grandma forced him to so I wouldn't be home alone.

Sure, he left out food for the dog—but what kind of person with a conscience wouldn't? And fine, he had set up the motorcycle sidecar so Bear could come with us out to the fire tower—but that was probably just so he wouldn't have to feel guilty about leaving me alone at the bottom of the fire tower stairs every day. And yes, he'd fed me ice cream for dinner—but that was driven by pure laziness.

"Fine," I said, settling into my usual spot on the rock at the base of the tower. "Enjoy your day."

Grandpa heaved a sigh and stood still, looming over me. After a few seconds of uncomfortable silence, he said, "Do you want me to help you try to climb up partway?" He was probably worried I'd complain to Grandma or something, and then he'd get in trouble for not being nice to me.

I shook my head. "No, thank you. I'm fine down here."

He sighed again and made his way toward the stairs. But

when he got to the bottom step, he sat down and looked at me. "How's your toe?"

I wiggled it inside my sock. To be honest, I hadn't really noticed it much the past few days. I'd actually kind of forgotten about it. "Better."

"Glad to hear it," he said.

Neither of us said anything for a while. I wondered how long he'd sit there out of guilt, before deciding it was time to escape up to his private little fortress.

Eventually, he broke the silence when he muttered, "I really should get up to work." I nodded and pressed my lips into a thin line, staring down at the dirt. Then, out of the blue, Grandpa Howard said, "You asked about my favorite job earlier?"

"Yeah." I glanced up, curious.

"This is it. Keeping watch in this tower." He whistled, and Bear hustled over to rub up against him. Grandpa reached his hand out, scratching behind the dog's ears. It was the first real sign of affection I'd seen from him since arriving in Thistledew. He went on, "I know they don't really need me up here nowadays. I'm not getting paid to do the job—it's just something I can't quite let go. Most fire lookouts in this neck of the woods have been closed up over the past few decades, but I'm not ready to call this one quits yet."

"Why?" I asked.

"That's a longer story," he said.

"I've got plenty of time, if you want to tell it," I offered.

Grandpa shook his head. "Nah." He stood up, startling Bear, who was in a trance from the ear rub. "Here's an idea—how about we try climbing a little ways up the tower steps together. You can take it one step at a time; try to get just part of the way up. Like that toe of yours, it might feel better and be easier to deal with if you've got someone beside you to lean on."

When he offered this, I felt intensely guilty. Partly because I'd *just* been thinking about how mean he was only a few minutes earlier. And now here he was, offering to help me try to fight my fear of heights. But I also felt guilty because, even with him beside me, I really didn't *want* to try to climb those stairs. What would climbing the fire tower get me? A few minutes of sheer terror, followed by even further terror that I'd actually spot a forest fire?

Ooh, goody.

But then I reminded myself: That was Old Maia, coming up with excuses. New Maia would be willing to go for it—to take a few steps at least, just to make an effort. "Okay," I said, standing up and brushing the pine needles and gravel off my jeans.

Grandpa took hold of my left arm and guided me toward the stairs. Bear flanked my right side. Together, with the two of them sandwiching me in for safety, I took a step up. We climbed slowly, and Grandpa talked the whole time. He told me about flowers that would start to come up among the grasses surrounding the tower within the next week and said that when the leaves grew in on the trees, it looked—to him—like an ocean of green waves from his perch inside the watchtower.

When we reached the first landing, Grandpa stopped. He helped me sit down with my back tight against the stair rail. Then he settled Bear down beside me, using one of the commands I'd taught him, and snapped to get him to rest his fluffy head in my lap. I was twenty feet off the ground, yet I found that I could still breathe. I hadn't been up this high since I'd let Amelia convince me to try one of the baby roller coasters at Six Flags last summer and nearly threw up from sheer terror while we were on the ride.

Now I let my eyes wander over the forest that was spread out before me. It was amazing how much of a difference twenty feet could make in how things looked. From up here, I could see tall birch trees swaying, black and white with tiny green leaf buds, on the edge of a small hill not too far off. An eagle or a hawk soared above the tops of the very same pine trees that we'd climbed through on our hike up the hill to the tower that morning. The sky looked expansive, massive, and it was easy to see that the forest went on for miles. I could only imagine what the view must be like from the very top, seven more stories up.

"This is far enough for today," Grandpa said. "You sit here, get used to how this feels, and we'll try to go a little farther another day."

"Okay," I said, grateful he wasn't going to push me. I smiled at him. "Thanks."

"You done good, kid."

"It's only twelve steps," I reminded him. "It's not like I climbed Mount Everest. Let's not get too excited."

Grandpa shrugged. "We all have our own Mount Everest, Maia. You just gotta climb yours one step at a time."

CHAPTER TWELVE

On Sunday morning, after church, Wendy offered to keep an eye on me while Grandma worked and Grandpa spent another day out at the fire tower. That way I could help Griffin with his Scout badge work while Wendy got a few chores done.

Griffin and I decided to set up our badge headquarters inside the cardboard fort. It still hadn't rained at all, so the fortress was in great shape. We dragged in a few pillows from the sofa, and a whole container of Oreos, and Griffin opened his spiral-bound badge book to study our options.

"Since we have all day," Griffin said, "I think we should work on one of the big ones."

"Like what?" I asked, munching on a double-decker Double Stuf Oreo. My sister had been the one to convince me to try eating an Oreo like this for the first time. She took one cookie off two Double Stuf Oreos, then smushed the cream parts together to make a double Double Stuf. I'm pretty sure there's no better food on Earth.

Griffin chewed the eraser on his pencil. "For Make It Move, we get to create an exploding craft stick reaction, build a pulley and a lever, and plan a Rube Goldberg machine." He glanced up at me and wiggled his eyebrows. "Do you know what a Rube Goldberg machine is?" he asked.

"I think so . . . ?" I lied. I was embarrassed to admit to a little kid that I'd *heard* the term, but I had never actually known what it was referring to.

I think Griffin suspected I was fibbing and tried to explain it to me. "Basically, there are all these separate things, right? Falling dominoes, water levers, pulleys, and whatever other stuff that work as a team to perform some simple task. Each step in the process triggers the next step and so on. If the design works right, it's super cool to see how all the different objects work together to do something really simple." He looked at me very seriously. "Get it?"

"Um . . . no."

"I think I'll have to just show you," he said, shaking his head.

"It sounds fun," I said.

"Well, now we know what we're doing today, then," Griffin announced. "Let's start by planning out our Rube Goldberg machine. If we're smart about it, we can just build the pulley, lever, and exploding thing into our plan for that. That way, we'll tick off all our badge requirements in one ultra-amazing project."

We each ate another Oreo, then set off to forage around in the shed in Grandma and Grandpa's backyard. That dilapidated old building seemed to be an endless source of everything we might need for any possible project. As Griffin pointed and directed me to gather up ropes, wood, a collection of small balls, a shovel, an old bird feeder, a bunch of crates, and a few other things, I asked him about school.

I was beginning to really miss my friends. I'd been removed from a lot of the group texts I was usually on, because people were planning events and get-togethers I couldn't be a part of, and some of my school friends had stopped sending me messages once they realized I wasn't ever going to write back. I never looked at Instagram anymore, and all the other social media stuff I used to waste time with just seemed stupid now. Beckett, Anne, Isabel, and June all checked in pretty regularly, but my closest friends seemed to be shielding me from regular daily stuff. Mostly, they just asked if I needed anything and wanted to know if I was okay, or if I wanted to talk. I appreciated the concern, but I still didn't want to talk about what had happened and also kinda just wished they would tell me if anything interesting had happened during the last few weeks of school. My regular life had started to fade into the background, and it was getting harder to imagine ever going back. How would I ever fit in there like I had before after so much had changed?

"I'm glad it's almost over," Griffin said, his face falling.

"Don't you like school?"

He shrugged. "Not really. I'm not very good at it."

"How is that possible?" I asked. "You're brilliant."

"Tell my teacher and my mom that," he said.

I tilted my head to one side, waiting for him to go on.

"Okay, so here's what I mean. I can memorize almost anything," he said, his arms loaded full of crates of supplies as we trundled out into the yard. "You can test me, even. My mom's grocery list, the Scouting badge requirements, the TV schedule, batting stats of every Twins player . . . but spelling words? I fail those tests, every week."

"But spelling tests are just simple memorization," I said.

"I know," he said, sighing. "And it's even worse in math. I look at all those numbers, and they just kind of jumble together into soup. My teacher told my mom I'm struggling and not up to grade level in half the stuff we're doing, and now she's all worried about me." He pushed out his lips and blew a raspberry. "Anyway, that's why I'm trying to finish all the Scout badges. I want her to know I'm good at *something*. She's really smart, my mom. But my dad, I guess he was kind of a dud." He cringed. "I heard my mom say that to your grandma one day—that my dad is a dud. It's kind of a funny word, but I don't think she meant it in a funny way."

"Yeah," I said, chewing my lower lip. "I think you're probably right."

"So if I finish all my badge work, I'll get honored at the fall den meeting and my mom will get to stand up when I'm presented with all those new patches. She'd like that—to see everyone clapping for me, celebrating her awesome son. My teacher's son is in Scouts, too, so she'll be at the meeting, and then she'll find out that I'm not bad at *everything*—just the things she makes me do."

I nodded. "Okay," I said. I could understand that. I'd felt the same way lately, too; I was desperate to show my parents how well I was handling my summer banishment to Thistledew. It would feel so good to have someone notice the things I was doing right. "That makes sense. But you do know *you're* not a dud, right, Griff?" I dumped my armload of supplies onto the ground in the backyard. Bear sniffed around at our collection, picked up an old tennis ball from the center of the pile, and trotted off to chew it on the other side of the yard.

"Of course I know that," Griffin said with a haughty sniff. "I just want to make sure everyone else knows it, too."

I laughed. "That's good."

Griffin and I stood quietly together for a minute and watched Bear, who was now tossing the ball into the air with his mouth and then chasing after it. It was probably the saddest, loneliest game of fetch I'd ever seen. "I just got an idea," Griffin said, grinning. "How about we make it so our Rube Goldberg machine throws that ball to Big Bear? Then he can be part of the project, too."

"That sounds complicated," I told him.

"You doubt me?" he asked, wiggling his eyebrows.

"If you say it can be done," I said, holding my hands up, "I believe you. Show me what I need to do."

• • •

It took all afternoon—and a trip to the Y Store to see Grandma, so we could each get a chocolate ice cream cone for energy and focus—but we did it. By the time Grandpa's motorcycle crunched onto the gravel in the driveway, Griffin and I had built, rebuilt, and successfully tested our Rube Goldberg machine at least several dozen times.

To get the process rolling, we had made a swinging

105

pulley out of rope and a tiny garden shovel. Once it was swinging, the shovel knocked a softball off the top of a pile of stacked-up wooden crates, sending it careening through a tube made of old, rusted metal downspouts that someone must have taken off the gutters on the house. The ball rolled out of the metal tube and knocked into a two-by-four scrap board, which set off a domino-style knockdown of even more two-by-fours. The final board kicked over a rake, which in turn crashed into a little red wagon. After being set in motion by the rake, the wagon rolled across the grass and slammed into a huge snow shovel that was hanging by its handle at one end of the clothesline. The shovel zipped down the slippery clothesline, acting just like a zip line. At the other end of the clothesline, the scoop on the shovel worked like a giant bat and thwacked into an old T-ball tee that had the tennis ball perched on top, ready to sail out into the yard.

It took a bunch of tries for us to get all the parts of our design to work fluidly together, and I was shocked that Griffin never got frustrated or gave up. He would just tinker, or ask me to fiddle with something, and then he'd think for a second before making a few adjustments that seemed to solve the problem almost perfectly the next time we tested it.

Bear was so excited when the whole thing worked out as it was supposed to. Whenever our Rube Goldberg machine worked without hitting any glitches, the shovel knocked into the ball with serious force and sent it flying for him to fetch on the other side of the yard. He'd chase after it, then bound back and stand in front of me or Griffin with the ball clutched in his teeth.

I couldn't wait to show Grandpa what we'd made. As soon as he'd parked the motorcycle, I called for him to come over. I met him just as he came around the side of the house. "Are you ready to see something amazing?" I asked, grinning madly.

Grandpa stood back, arms crossed over his chest.

"Drumroll, please!" Griffin called out.

I tapped my hands on my thighs, the closest thing I could get to a drumroll sound.

Then Griffin swung the little metal shovel and set our Rube Goldberg machine into motion. First the shovel pulley, then the ball slide, the wooden dominoes, rake to wagon to zip line. Everything went exactly according to design. When the shovel slid down the clothesline and thwacked into the tennis ball, Bear scurried after it, collected the ball, and returned it—dripping with saliva—to Grandpa's feet.

"Ta-da!" I exclaimed. "Griffin and I designed the whole thing ourselves. Isn't it impressive?"

Grandpa poked the tennis ball with his foot, nudging it away. "That sure is something," he said, in the same tone of voice he might use if we'd successfully colored a page in a coloring book or put on matching socks. It was a little annoying that his level of enthusiasm did not match our level of engineering mastery. But if I'd learned anything about

Grandpa since arriving in Minnesota, it was that he didn't waste words just for the sake of saying something.

And even though he didn't say it out loud, I could tell he was impressed.

But I guess more importantly? *I* was proud of us, and sometimes that mattered even more.

. . .

As soon as Griffin left for dinner and his forced Sunday-night shower, I called my parents to check in.

"We stopped by the house with some friends today," Mom told me. "To see if there was anything we could salvage out of the ruins of the fire."

Dad jumped in behind her on the screen. "Almost all of your and Amelia's baby and toddler pictures survived the fire!"

"Thank goodness we moved them into our bedroom during the basement construction," Mom added, her smile looking more real than it had all week. "We were also able to pull out a few kitchen appliances that should be usable, and the dining room table somehow looks okay."

I let out a breath I hadn't realized I'd been holding in. I guess I'd started to assume that every piece of our old lives was gone. Knowing that a few pictures, the fridge, and the dining room table—where my sister and I did all our homework and played table football and made our Play-Doh feasts—had made it through the fire was oddly comforting. It didn't sound like much of the house structure was intact or safe to walk in, so my parents were working with the insurance people to figure out what our options were. Either we'd try to fix what remained, or they would have to tear it all down and build a new house from the ground up. Mom and Dad had been staying with friends and sleeping mostly in the hospital for the first week after the fire, but now they were living in an Extended Stay America hotel room.

"It's a good thing you're not here," Dad said lightly, obviously trying to make me feel better about everything I'd been missing. "Our room just has one double bed, and the TV options are not great."

"That's too bad," I said.

"Eh," Dad said. "We're not there much. Just to shower and change and take a nap, or take turns grabbing a full night's sleep every once in a while." He settled into the chair in the corner of my sister's hospital room, since Mom had moved out of the frame. He asked, "So what's new with you? We miss you, Maia."

I had been waiting for him to ask, so I could tell them all about the past few days. Even though I hadn't made it any farther up the fire tower that week, I *did* actually make it into the water at swim lessons on Thursday. Griffin and I had made a pact that we would try to do everything our teacher Evan thought we were ready to do. Which is how we ended up wading out until we were each shoulder-deep in the water. Then we picked up our feet and let our bodies dangle in the lake, making it feel like we didn't have solid ground below us anymore. Maybe it was wearing the life jacket, or maybe it was the promise to myself that I'd *try* to shed some of my fears and help Griffin during our lessons, but I actually did it. And I could even imagine floating out in the lake someday—or bobbing around, playing catch in the deep end of the pool with my friends—without a life jacket. I'd never realized how much I wanted to do those things until they actually felt like a real possibility.

I'd been so excited to tell them about all of that, and the view from the first landing on the fire tower, and how I was teaching Bear how to be a pet, and me and Griffin's Rube Goldberg creation. But mostly, I'd been eager to show Mom and Dad how well I was handling things—getting brave, even—so maybe they would see that I was ready to come home.

But almost as soon as Dad asked his question, a doctor came into the room to chat with my parents about another skin grafting procedure Amelia was having done later in the week. Skin grafting, I'd recently learned, is where they take healthy skin from one part of my sister's body and use it to help heal some of the most severely burned areas. She'd already gone through a few of these surgeries, but Amelia had more of them ahead of her, and I knew my parents had a lot of questions. With an apology and a promise to talk tomorrow, Dad hustled off the phone, so I didn't get to tell them anything at all.

CHAPTER THIRTEEN

On Monday morning, another fire nightmare woke me up early, before Grandpa knocked to tell me it was time to get a move on. After I'd gotten dressed and brushed my teeth, I scrubbed the edges of the dream out of my mind by singing songs from Disney movies aloud.

As I grabbed hold of my breakfast bag (mini pumpkin muffins!) and shuffled down the stairs and out the door, I realized that, for the first time since we'd started this crazy routine, I was actually kind of looking forward to getting back to the fire tower. Something about the new regularity of me and Grandpa's daily outing brought a strange kind of comfort in a time that had been filled with uncertainty. I loved my morning ride on the back of Grandpa's cycle, and after a few weeks of listening to the same awful music over and over again, I sometimes caught myself humming along to a few of his funny country songs.

I was tired from me and Griffin's busy weekend and the terrible dreams that had continued to plague my sleep, so almost as soon as we hit the far end of town that morning, I started to drift off. My helmeted head rested between Grandpa's shoulder blades and I let myself sink into a dreamless sleep. I'm not sure how long I was dozing, but I was shaken awake suddenly when the motorcycle rolled and tilted, and I was certain we were about to spill right off the road.

"Pops!" I screamed, getting a tighter hold on his flannel shirt. I could feel Grandpa's chest and body shaking where I had my arms wrapped around him, so I grabbed hold of his shoulder, hard, and yelled, "Are you okay?"

A moment later, the motorcycle eased onto the shoulder and we turned down our regular road to the trail. Grandpa slowed down and brought the cycle to a stop. I jumped off and stood beside him, certain my pops was having a heart attack or a seizure or something. Bear barked, alarmed by my sudden and abrupt movements. But when Grandpa pulled off his helmet, I saw that he was chuckling.

"What's funny?" I shrieked. "Why are you laughing? Are you dying?"

"Sorry, kid," he said, looking not at all sorry. "I'm fine. I could tell you'd fallen asleep back there, and I didn't want you to sink so deep that you fell off the back. So I did a little swerve, hoping to wake you. Didn't think it would scare the pants off you quite the way it did."

"What were you thinking?" I hissed. "You could have gotten us both killed! What if the motorcycle had tipped over?"

"By swerving?" Grandpa asked, chuckling. "Swerving's what I gotta do to avoid hitting turtles and potholes on the road. Motorcycles are *built* for swerving. We weren't in any danger."

"What if you'd swerved *me* right off the back of the motorcycle?" I huffed, growing increasingly agitated. "I mean, I could easily have lost my hold on you and just slid onto the highway. What then?"

"Then you wouldn't be feeling so great right about now," he replied matter-of-factly. "But I *didn't* knock you off the bike, so seems like all's well."

"But—" I sputtered. "What if—"

"You're just fine, kid," he said, no longer laughing. "Calm yourself. No sense getting so worked up over what could have happened, when we already know everything turned out okay."

I'd begun to realize this was the biggest way Grandpa and I were different. I preferred to be ready for every worst-case scenario so I'd be prepared for whatever bad stuff came my way. Pops, on the other hand, seemed to be firmly in the camp of believing that "whatever happens, happens," no matter if or how you prepare.

"Fine," I huffed. "But don't do that ever again."

Grandpa held up his hands, palms open toward me, as a gesture of apology. "Understood," he said. "I thought it was kinda funny. But I guess I was wrong."

I schlumped back toward the motorcycle. "It was maybe a little funny," I grumbled. Then, for good measure, I added, "But just so you know, steering violently so you swerve all over the highway on a motorcycle is not a nice way to wake someone up."

"Won't happen again," Grandpa muttered. He chuckled some more and said, "Did you hear your scream? You can yell, kid."

Grandpa started up the cycle and drove—without further incident—the rest of the way to the fire tower access trail.

"I'm sorry I overreacted," I said as we grabbed our packs and started our hike up. "I don't know, I guess I just—"

"Quit dwelling on it," Grandpa interrupted. "Not worth gettin' worked up about any further. What's done is done." In a quiet voice, he added, "You gotta move on and let it go."

"Yeah," I said, nodding. "Yeah, okay."

I don't know if he was talking about the swerve, or about the fire. Really, he could have been talking about anything in my life. But while we walked, I let what he said sink in. *Move on and let it go . . .*

By the time we reached the tower, I felt okay. Not perfect, but better.

"Can we try going a little farther up the stairs today?" I asked Grandpa.

"Sure thing," Grandpa said, not making a big deal of it. He just pulled the biggest mini muffin out of the breakfast bag, handed it to me, and headed toward the bottom of the stairs. He and Bear set up shop on the bottom step and looked at me. "We'll head up whenever you're ready."

• • •

I made it almost as far as the tower's second stair landing that morning. While I climbed, I kept expecting that familiar sick feeling to hit me, the need to throw up from nerves and fear, but for the first time in as long as I could remember, the feeling didn't come. As we trudged up the rickety metal steps, Grandpa reminded me to keep breathing, and to not look down or back—to just focus on what was ahead of me. By the time I collapsed onto the little platform two stories up, I had worked up a bit of a sweat, but I was still able to breathe and I couldn't even taste vomit at the back of my throat.

I was still only a quarter of the way to the top, but it felt like I'd already summited a mountain. Maybe it was just me, but I'm pretty sure the air felt thinner this high up. I could see even farther out over the valley, and I was starting to understand why the Forest Service had set up lookouts like this back in the day to spot fires. You really could see for miles, and I knew firsthand that with fire, every second counted.

While Grandpa climbed the rest of the way up to his perch at the top, Big Bear and I sat on that second landing and got used to the view. I already knew I was going to need help getting back down to solid ground again, but I'd made it this far without completely freaking out—which was a big step. I was pretty sure this was higher than the kiddie coaster Amelia had dragged me onto at Six Flags. It was certainly much higher than the top of the zip line at the pool. I wished Amelia and my friends could see the view from way up here. I wished they could see *me* way up here.

By the time we hiked back down the trail at the end of the day, I was feeling pretty good about myself. But because it took a while for me to climb down all those stairs, it was a little later than usual when we hopped on the motorcycle to head home. Grandma had promised us hamburgers for dinner, so I was eager to get back to town. She made really good hamburgers, and almost always served them with canned green beans—dripping with melted butter—that Grandpa had grown in his garden last summer.

While we zoomed down the highway, I let myself relax in the warm, dry, late-afternoon sun. We passed Smokey Bear and his sign, which now read FIRE DANGER: HIGH. The sun had already dropped below the tree line, and the road was almost empty of cars. But then, suddenly, we came around a wide, sweeping corner and found a car stopped in the middle of the road. There were skid marks, and the car's driver was standing on the side of the road, looking bewildered.

Grandpa eased the cycle onto the shoulder and approached the driver. As he walked toward the woman, I noticed something behind them, heaped up on the side of the road. Curious, I climbed off the back of the motorcycle, told Bear to stay, and made my way toward Grandpa and the woman.

The woman was talking fast, her hands moving like leaves in the breeze, and she was obviously upset. Grandpa was soothing her, his voice calmer and gentler than I was accustomed to. By the time I reached them, the woman had started walking back to her car. Before I could find out what was going on, the woman drove off. Her car made funny clanking noises, but it seemed to be moving just fine.

Once she was gone, I realized what she'd left behind: a deer, obviously dead, on the side of the road.

"She hit it square on," Grandpa told me. "That's what you're

116

supposed to do. You don't swerve, or else it's likely you'll both end up dead."

I stared at that deer, crumpled up on the side of the road. I didn't need to touch it or even get close to know it was still warm. Blood oozed out the side of the poor animal's face, and its legs were splayed at an unnatural angle. "It's dead," I said quietly, stating the obvious.

"Thank God," Grandpa said.

"*Thank God?*" I blurted out, incredulous.

"It could be worse," he told me. "Could have been severely injured and suffering. But at that point, she'd be nothing more than food for the wolves. Or, worse yet, the lady in the car could be dead in the ditch. Better that the car didn't go off the road, the deer got hit clear on, and died right away without any pain."

I stared at him as he studied the dead deer on the shoulder, seemingly without any care or concern at all for the fact that a life had been lost. "How can you say that?" I asked.

"It's a fact of life, Maia," he said. "We all die eventually."

"You're acting like it's not a big deal that this deer is dead!" I said, growing more and more frustrated with Grandpa's lack of compassion. "It was just going about its business, crossing from one patch of grass to the next, and it got bowled over by some lady who was probably driving too fast. It's not fair." Tears had begun to stream down my face. "If we'd left at our regular time, maybe *we* would have hit it, or scared it away from the road, or kept that lady from being

117

on the wrong part of the road at the exact wrong time. Or maybe, if it was us who came upon it, you would have *swerved* and we would have missed it altogether, and everyone could have gone on with their regular lives."

"Kid, you gotta learn that you can't prevent all bad things from happening, and you definitely can't change the things that have already happened," Grandpa replied matter-of-factly. "But what you *can* do is make the best of a bad situation."

"And what's the *best* in this situation?" I asked, growing even more hysterical. "Huh? We drag the dead deer off the side of the road and leave it for wolves to gnaw on as soon as we drive away?"

"Well," he said, considering. "That's the first thing we ought to do. We don't want someone else to hit it and then have them careening off the road, do we?"

I crossed my arms over my chest. He had a point, but I was still angry. How could he be so heartless? Wasn't he at all sad?

Grandpa reached down to pull at the deer's hind legs. But after he'd dragged it just a couple of feet off onto the shoulder of the highway, he stood up and shook his head.

"What?" I huffed. "Why are you shaking your head?"

"I'm tryin' to figure out what to do about this situation," he said, and hustled over to the motorcycle. All this time, Bear had been sitting, nice and still, strapped into the harness in his sidecar. But now, as Grandpa approached, he began wagging his tail and whining, eager to get out and run. I followed Grandpa, knowing the old guy wouldn't bother to pat Bear or reassure him that everything was okay.

As I stroked our big dog's ears, Grandpa hastily rustled around in the compartment of stuff attached to the back of the cycle. After digging way down to the bottom, he pulled out a giant knife in a leather holster thing. "Now what are you doing?" I gasped. I braced myself, waiting for him to tell me he was going to cut up the deer for meat or something.

"This deer's pregnant," he said, scrambling down onto his knees beside the dead creature's belly. "I'm pretty sure her baby might still be alive in there, and based on her size, it looks like it could be about full term. We've gotta get that calf out quick if we want to try to save a life." He fixed me with a serious look. "Now, I know you're squeamish about stuff—how do you do with blood?"

I hated blood. Whenever Amelia or I scraped a knee, or Dad cut his finger while chopping veggies, I felt all the blood rush out of my face and the whole world tunneled. But if there was a baby inside this deer's belly, and we had a chance to pull it out and give it a life, well . . . "I'm fine," I said. "I'll be fine."

Before I had a chance to change my answer, Grandpa had bent over the dead deer and begun carefully slicing open her abdomen. I averted my eyes, but when Grandpa told me he needed a hand, I dropped down on the gravel beside him, reached my hands into the dead animal's belly, and helped

Grandpa pull out a squirming mass of baby deer. It wriggled and writhed, alive in his arms. There was goo and blood everywhere, but I hardly noticed.

"That's all right now," Grandpa cooed, cuddling the deer close to keep it warm. It was a bony mass of long legs, spotted wet fur, and the sweetest face I'd ever seen. Pops winked and gave me a little smile before turning his attention back to the helpless newborn critter. Suddenly, Grandpa looked a lot less heartless to me than he had a few minutes before. "It's gonna be all right."

CHAPTER FOURTEEN

We flagged down a car that was heading into town, and Grandpa asked if he could borrow their phone so we could call Grandma to give us a ride. She showed up ten minutes later with a cardboard box and a blanket to wrap up the newborn deer and keep her warm inside a makeshift bed. Grandpa let me carry the box to the car. I was surprised at how light the little animal was. It couldn't have been more than five or six pounds, about the size of a tiny human newborn. I walked slowly and carefully, then gently placed the baby box in the back seat before settling in beside it. Grandma drove me and the calf into town while Grandpa followed behind with Big Bear on the cycle.

Grandpa dropped Bear off at home, then disappeared while Grandma and I got the fawn settled into a corner of the shed. Grandma dragged a few more blankets out of the basement to cover the hard, dirty floor, and I cleared away anything that looked sharp or at risk of falling on the little fawn in the night.

When Grandpa Howard returned from wherever he'd gone, he found me tucked into a corner of the shed with my legs curled around the deer to help keep it warm. He was holding a baby bottle in one hand and a big bag full of hay in the other. He looked at me and the calf for a moment, then held the bottle toward me and said, "You need to get her to drink this special formula."

"Me?"

"Looks like she trusts you," he said, squatting down beside me. He started shaking hay out onto the floor of the shed, creating a fresh, soft bed for the calf to lie on. "I talked to my friend over at the Department of Natural Resources to see what we gotta do to help this critter out now that her mama's gone. We have to get this special stuff in her body as soon as possible. It's similar to the milk she would have gotten from her mother within the first hour or so after she was born, and it's filled with all kinds of nutrients and vitamins that will help keep her from getting sick. If she survives the night, then tomorrow we'll start her on goat's milk or a deer milk alternative. But tonight is gonna be critical to keeping her alive."

I gazed down at the tiny critter, now settled into a tight circle surrounded by hay and blankets. Her soft brown coat with the milky white spots, the little rib bones you could see outlined through her velvety hide. Curled up in the shed, unaware that she'd been left all alone to make her way in the world. This creature was relying on me to keep her alive through her first night, and there was absolutely no way I was going to let someone die on my watch. I grabbed the bottle from Grandpa and nudged it against the little fawn's mouth. She moved her lips around but seemed confused about what was happening.

Grandpa helped me adjust how I held the bottle, and together we kept trying to get her to drink. The calf wanted nothing except to sleep. The poor little thing—safe and sound and snuggly inside her mother's belly one minute, pulled out into the world by a pair of human hands the next. I shook the bottle, easing a little of the fluid out of the nipple until it dripped onto her face. Grandpa reached forward, touching the calf, and did something that made the fawn's mouth open just the tiniest bit. As soon as it was open, I sprinkled a few drops of the liquid onto her tongue. She squirmed, her mouth moving awkwardly as she tried to swallow it down. After a few more drops like this, she reached out and put her mouth to the bottle's nipple. She picked and prodded at it at first, but then she took it in her mouth and slowly began to nurse.

She only swallowed a few tiny drops, but Grandpa said it was a good first effort. "Just like you up at the fire tower," he said. "We gotta start slow. Ease her into it. This is all new to her." According to Grandpa's friend at the DNR, who I guess knew about these sorts of things, we were supposed to feed her every four hours for the first few days. But he promised it would get easier once she got the hang of the bottle and started to actually feel hungrier without us telling her it was time to drink.

That night, Grandma and Grandpa let me carry a sleeping bag out to the shed and sleep beside the fawn. Bear sat right outside the door of the shed, instinctively protecting both me and the baby deer from any would-be intruders. Grandma brought me a sandwich and a bowl of ice cream, and took over watch duties while I ran inside to brush my teeth and use the bathroom.

As soon as I returned to the shed, I snuggled into my sleeping bag, nestled in right beside the fawn's pile of hay and blankets, and studied the sleepy baby in the hazy evening light, making sure she didn't look sick, sad, or in any discomfort. The little fawn just looked asleep. Luckily, I could see her ribs moving a fraction of an inch every few seconds, so I knew she wasn't dead or anything. I was worried that's what would happen—that she would just up and die, and suddenly I'd be lying there next to a dead animal. I wasn't sure, based on what Grandpa had said, how likely it was that she'd survive the night. She seemed to be doing all right to me, but I knew literally nothing about baby deer.

I lay there in the dark, musty shed, reaching out to touch the deer's flank every five minutes or so. I could hear Grandpa going in and out of his camper door in the yard, but eventually things quieted outside. Bear began to snore and snuffle in his sleep, which was how I knew he hadn't left his post. I could hear an owl hooting—low, somber, mournful—somewhere out in the woods behind the house. But otherwise, the world was still, and I let myself relax and think about what I'd done that afternoon. I had climbed partway up a fire tower and helped my grandpa birth a baby deer. How many kids from my school at home in Chicago could say that? I think it was safe to guess a grand total of *none*. My sister would love this story, and I could already predict she'd make me tell it over and over again, until every last detail was set to memory, making it impossible for me to forget this day as long as I lived.

Eventually, I fell asleep. Several times in the night, I woke to the sound of movement. Once, I looked over and saw the fawn shifting inside her haystack. I sat up, worried. For the hundredth time, I touched the side of her bony body to be sure she was still breathing. She was. I picked up the bottle and offered her a drink. She played with the nipple and took it gingerly in her mouth, drinking a little of the special formula down. After she'd tired of the effort of drinking from the human baby bottle, she let out a soft breath and settled into sleep again.

Later in the night, I heard something at the door. I peeked through half-closed eyes and caught Grandpa sneaking in to check on us. He'd come with a fresh bottle, and while I pretended to sleep, he crouched down beside the two of us and offered the fawn more food. In the light of the moon, which snuck in through the half-open shed door, I saw a look on his face that was impossible not to understand—a mix of love, compassion, and concern. In that moment, I decided Grandpa Howard was magnificent. No one could look at a newborn fawn that way and *not* be something special. I fell asleep to the sound of Grandpa clucking and cooing at the deer, urging her to take just a few more sips.

By some miracle, the fawn made it through the night. I woke to find her mewling beside me. Grandpa arrived almost instantly, passing me yet another bottle. I pressed it toward the deer's mouth, and this time, she took it immediately. She gummed at the nipple, then began to suck. She pulled away a few times, overwhelmed by the heavy flow of milk from the man-made bottle, but she had obviously already gotten the hang of it. She drank eagerly, filling her empty belly with food and nutrients.

I was relieved that she was eating, but sad that she'd never met her mother or the rest of her family. In one split second, her whole life had shifted course. Was it better, I wondered, to never know how things would have been if life had played out differently? Was it easier not to have to mourn the things you never knew you'd lost?

That morning, Grandpa stuck around the house longer than usual. Grandma got someone to cover her shift at work so that I didn't have to go out to the fire tower and could keep the fawn's feeding schedule somewhat regular. Grandpa left around nine but told me he'd set up a few visits throughout the day from friends he knew from his Forest Service days. They had offered to swing by and give us some tips and advice on raising the calf. He'd also called some lady he knew, a vet with wildlife experience, and asked her to stop by to give the calf a quick once-over. Apparently, the Forest Service people had suggested that we send the fawn to a wildlife rehabilitation center, but Grandpa had adamantly refused.

"I've got some experience with this sort of thing, and she's going to get plenty of personal attention and care here," he grumbled while we were working together to set up a little fenced area just out the door of the shed. The fawn would apparently spend most of her first few weeks sleeping and lying around, but we wanted her to have a safe place to roam when she did decide to get up and stretch her legs. "We're her family now, and a family's job is to take care of each other when bad stuff happens."

I was thankful Grandpa had decided not to send the calf away. I'd gotten attached and felt responsible for her well-being. Bear had already proven he was a charming gentleman by keeping his distance and protecting our little guest, so the new kid was fitting in well.

Around lunchtime, after her second feeding of the day and several visits from Forest Service folks and the friendly vet, the fawn decided to test out her legs and walk around a little for the first time since we'd pulled her from her mother's womb. She stumbled a bit as she got to her feet, but then she took a few shaky steps across the shed. She ambled out into the tiny yard we'd set up for her and took in her surroundings. After less than a minute, her legs gave out again and she plopped down on the soft grass. I sat crisscross applesauce and studied her, watching the way she breathed, listening to the sweet little mewling sounds she made, admiring her knobby limbs that seemed too long for her tiny body. The sun beat down on the grass, warming us both. After a moment, her eyes drifted closed and she settled into a relaxed sleep. Bear came over to sniff her over the short fencing. He gently pressed his nose against her body, verifying that she was all right, and then lay down—right beside her—on the other side of the fence.

Grandma came outside every once in a while to deliver an apple or some cheese and crackers. At one point, she carried a tray with Kool-Aid for me, a dish of fresh water for Bear, and a fresh bottle for the calf. The three of us were still there, relaxing in and around the fenced deer pen a few hours later when Griffin got off the school bus. He bounded down the lane, whooping and hollering a greeting to me and Bear. Unlike most days, Bear didn't run to greet him—it was obvious that he wasn't willing to leave his new sister unprotected. I waved Griffin over, watching his expression shift when he noticed the tiny newborn critter curled up in the corner of the pen.

"What—is—that?" he gasped. I told him the story of what had happened, and Griffin listened intently. Then he whispered, "Can I . . . touch it?"

"Sure," I said. "If there were any chance her mother was still alive, we wouldn't want to touch her so as not to alter her scent or get in the way of her mother feeding and raising her properly," I explained. "But since her mom is dead, and we're the best hope she has for survival, all the usual rules for handling wildlife are off."

Griffin climbed over the fence, settling down on his knees to touch the fawn's velvety ear. Bear whined, begging to come inside the pen with us, but Grandpa and I had already decided it was best if we kept the two of them apart until we knew the calf was thriving. Griffin looked at me curiously. "Since when are you an expert in raising deer?"

I laughed. "A vet and some people from the Forest Service and the DNR came by today to look her over. Until then, I knew nothing."

Griffin ran his finger gently over her rib cage. "She's so tiny," he said reverently. "What's her name?"

"I haven't named her yet," I told him. "I was waiting for you."

"For *me*?" Griffin looked like I'd just awarded him with a pot of gold, not naming rights to an orphaned deer. "Are you serious?"

"You gave Big Bear the perfect name," I told him. "What do you think fits her?"

Griffin's face shifted into his thinking expression. "Well . . ." he said, his eyes shifting upward to look at the sky. "I'm thinking: Wilma."

I snorted out a laugh. "Wilma?"

"Like Wilbur, from *Charlotte's Web*. But a girl. Wilma."

"Wilma," I repeated, testing it out. "It's perfect."

Griffin bent down and cooed into the fawn's ear. "Hello, Wilma. Welcome to Thistledew."

CHAPTER FIFTEEN

That night, Grandma told me it was time for me to move back inside and sleep in the den again. She and Grandpa had discussed it and thought it best if Wilma didn't get used to having me next to her while she slept, since I wouldn't be able to sleep out in the shed forever. I felt okay about moving inside and leaving her out there, because I knew Grandpa was out there, with the windows of his trailer wide open in case Wilma started wailing.

But as soon as I was back inside, the nightmares returned. I didn't know if it was because I had Wilma with me in the shed, giving me something else to focus on and care for, that made me feel free from some of my other worries and guilt and fears. All I knew was I had slept fitfully and dreamlessly the previous night, but now that I was able to fall more soundly asleep and didn't have either Bear or Wilma beside me, a fresh chapter of my normal nightmare returned in full force. That night, Amelia and I were both surrounded by flames. We were huddled together in the center of her bed, with flames licking at us from all sides. Suddenly, Amelia's hair caught fire and she flung herself off the bed, trying to stop, drop, and roll. I watched as she was consumed by the flames, screaming defenselessly as the fire chewed and swallowed her up.

My arms wouldn't move. I just watched, helpless, as my sister burned.

The room exploded in flames, and still I just sat on my little bed island, watching as everything around me went up in smoke.

Amelia was gone, and it was all my fault.

I woke up sweating, my breath coming quick and shallow. The red numbers on the clock told me it was 12:34. This was the hour Amelia always called "Number Time"— she even made up a little song and dance to commemorate one-two-three-four in a row on the clock. I sat up, searching for Astrid. But as soon as I scooped her up, the remnant smoke smell nearly choked me and soon I was hyperventilating, unable to get anything more than the tiniest sip of air.

All I could think in the moment was, I needed to breathe. I had more than six hours left of nighttime, and I couldn't imagine falling back to sleep with those images printed on my mind. I wanted to talk to my sister, to see her, to know that she was okay. But I couldn't.

Without thinking, I jumped out of bed and ran. I raced across the kitchen, scrambled down the stairs, and shoved open the door to the outside. Feet still bare, I rushed across the yard. Bear looked up sleepily from his perch at the outer edge of Wilma's fence, his tail thumping out a tired greeting. I rubbed his fluffy shoulders, immediately feeling a bit better, then peeked in at the fawn. She was fast asleep, so I stepped across the threshold into the shed, reaching in to gently touch her silky flank. I knelt down and let my hand rest on her warm body for a moment, forcing myself to match my own breathing to the slow, rhythmic up-and-down movement of her rib cage.

Once my breathing had calmed, I went back outside and stood in the yard. I could hear crickets, or cicadas, or some sort of squeaky bug making music in the dark of night, followed by the squeak of Grandpa's trailer door. I turned to see him silhouetted in the doorway. There was a dim light glowing somewhere inside the camper trailer and Grandpa was wearing his usual flannel and tan pants, so I couldn't tell if he was still awake at this hour, or if he slept in his clothes.

"Hi," I said.

"You're up early," he noted.

"You're up late."

"I don't sleep much," Grandpa said. "Need about four or five hours and then I'm done. That's why I sleep out here in the camper—your grandmother, she gets mad at me for coming in to bed so late and tossing and turning all night."

"Oh," I said softly. "Okay. I was wondering."

"What's up, kid?"

"I woke up and wanted to make sure Wilma was okay," I said, digging my toes into the dry, dead grass beneath my feet, trying to ground myself. My pinkie toe still throbbed a bit from time to time, but tonight I kind of wanted to bring on the pain. It would distract me from the nightmare. "I had another bad dream."

Grandpa let his camper door swing closed behind him and strode over to me on the lawn. "I'm sorry."

"It's not your fault," I pointed out. "I just couldn't sleep after, so I thought I'd check on her. And Bear always makes me feel a little better when I'm homesick and stuff."

"Do you want some hot cocoa?" Grandpa asked. "Might help you get back to sleep."

"I don't want to get back to sleep."

"Maia," he said, his voice gentle but firm. "You need to sleep. I know the dreams aren't easy, but they're probably helping you work through something."

"It's not something I want to work through," I muttered, surprised that Grandpa was actually trying to talk to me for once. But nothing had changed since those first few forced therapy sessions with Doctor Dan at the hospital after the fire. I didn't want to talk about it or think about it or rehash it. None of those things would change what had happened. Maybe the dreams were my mind's way of punishing me for what I'd done. Just like spending the summer in Thistledew—it's what I deserved after all I'd done and not done the night of the fire.

Grandpa sighed. "Do you want to sleep out here in the camper tonight?" he offered. "Maybe a change of scenery will help you shake them off?"

"Is there *room* for me in there?" Since arriving, I'd gotten the impression that the camper was Grandpa's domain. He'd never opened the door and let me in, had never suggested I take a look around. So I'd stayed away from his little room, giving him the space and privacy I knew he wanted and needed. But now he was opening the door and inviting me in.

"I can put a mat down," he said. "It's not the Comfort Suites, but it's better than sitting out here all night."

"Okay," I said, and followed Grandpa into the camper. The space inside looked pretty much exactly how I had guessed it would. There was a single bed, a small table, and a little kitchenette area with a hot plate and some containers of nuts, as well as a big bag of M&M's and a bunch of peanut brittle. "What are those for?" I asked, pointing at the candy as I slid into the narrow bench seat on one side of the tiny table.

"I snack when I can't sleep," he said.

"A healthy choice," I teased.

"Don't start." He tossed the package of M&M's my way, saying, "Peanut brittle's bad for your teeth. But help yourself to the chocolate."

Grandpa pulled a camping mat out from his under-bed storage area and rolled it out on the dirty floor. "You can take the bed," he said. "I'll sleep down here on the floor tonight."

"I'm not going to steal your bed," I told him.

"It's good for my back," Grandpa said. "Bed's too soft."

I had a feeling he wasn't going to change his mind, and he probably wanted me to drop it rather than bickering about it, so I said, "Okay."

"You like cocoa?" he asked, flipping on an electric water kettle. Only then did I realize that he'd strung an extension cord from the garage or the house out to the camper, which was how he had electricity.

"Sure," I said.

While Grandpa poured a few spoonfuls of chocolate powder into two mugs, I studied the nearly empty space. The only piece of art on the walls was an old black-and-white photograph: two teenagers with their arms slung around each other's shoulders. "Who's that?" I asked, pointing to the photo.

"Me and my brother," Grandpa said.

"Is he older or younger than you?"

"Older," he said, pouring steaming hot water into each of our cups.

"Does he live around here?" I asked. I was trying to remember my mom talking about an uncle, but honestly, she and Dad didn't talk much about either of their families. We saw Gram and Papa, Dad's parents, at Thanksgiving and for a week in the summer most years. And we only saw Mom's parents once each year, when they came to visit us in Chicago. Our lives were always just so crazy, and we had some pretty close friends in Chicago, so we never really took a lot of trips to see *actual* family. We had a family of friends close to home.

"No, he doesn't live around here," Grandpa said. He blew on his cocoa, obviously not willing to expand on his answer. "So tell me about these nightmares."

"Can I not?" I asked. "I'd rather just try to forget about the dream, if that's okay."

"Sure."

We sipped our cocoa in silence for a while. The space

inside the camper was cozy and quiet, like a little cave set apart from the rest of the world. I could see why Grandpa snuck off to this space each night. Even if it was partially true that Grandma had banished him from the bedroom, I had a feeling he liked having this space to get away.

"Actually, can I tell you something?" I said quietly, about halfway through my cocoa.

"If you want," Grandpa said.

"I could have gotten Amelia out of the fire sooner," I said, laying the confession out there without any apology, explanation, or comment. I decided to start there, rather than hitting him with the fact that I'd also *started* the fire with my own carelessness.

"Why do you think that?" he asked.

"I panicked," I told him. "I got scared, and I wasted all kinds of time when I could have been helping her escape."

Grandpa sat there for a long time, not saying anything. He rolled an orange back and forth across the table, beneath his open palm. The motion soothed me, lulled me into a false sense of comfort and calm. "You can't blame yourself, Maia."

"Yes, I can," I snapped. "And I do. I should."

"That's false."

"And that's where you and I will have to agree to disagree," I argued.

"Listen, kid," Grandpa said softly. "What's done is done. You've got to allow for self-forgiveness. Otherwise, the guilt's gonna eat you alive. Believe me."

"I can't," I whispered. "If I hadn't frozen in the moment,

Amelia wouldn't be stuck in a hospital bed right now, fighting for her life."

Grandpa looked up. "You're not doing anyone any good by thinking that way."

I didn't answer. I knew that was probably true, but it didn't make me feel any less guilty. "I just want to go home," I said. "I want my life back. I know it's not fair to you and Grandma to say that, since you've both been so nice to take me in this summer, but I want to go home. I want to be with my sister, and I want to help my parents clean up the house, and I don't want them all to forget I'm part of the family."

Grandpa sighed. He stood up and patted the bed, telling me in no uncertain terms that it was time to shut off for the night. "Sometimes," he said slowly as I climbed under the covers, "the best thing you can do is spend some time figuring out what it is that other people need and want. Because that isn't always exactly the same as what *you* need or want. And then you gotta decide, at this moment in time, which of those things matters more?"

I thought about that for a second. I knew what *I* wanted, and what I was pretty sure I *needed* more than anything, was to be home with my family while my sister healed. I wanted to help build our life back up, to fix all the things I'd broken on the night of the fire. I looked at Grandpa and said, "I guess what Mom and Dad need right now is time to focus on my sister and putting our lives back together?" He tilted his head, which I took as his way of saying yes.

What I *didn't* say out loud was, I figured they needed time to focus on those two things without having to worry about fixing me, too. Maybe if I had been a different kind of kid— the kind who was strong, with a hard shell and the courage to match—they wouldn't have had to ship me off while they handled the hard stuff. But that *wasn't* me, and so Mom and Dad had no choice. I'd brought this on myself.

Which meant I had to spend the rest of this summer focusing on who I wanted to be—*needed* to be, for my sister—so I could go home a better version of myself. Because if I couldn't change what had happened that night, at least I could make sure I never let something like this happen again.

STAGES OF A FIRE

STAGE 3: FULLY DEVELOPED (TRANSITION)

When the growth stage has reached its peak and all
combustible materials have been ignited and are being
consumed, a fire is considered fully developed. This is the
hottest and most dangerous phase of a fire.

CHAPTER SIXTEEN

Griffin had finally finished school for the year, so I could no longer deny that summer had well and truly arrived—and I hadn't yet been invited home. Over the past week, I'd finally started texting a little more with some of my friends to get end-of-year updates and catch up on the latest scoop from the real world. Then I made a few tentative calls, because talking—even just a little bit—with Grandpa after my bad middle-of-the-night dream had helped me figure some stuff out.

During a three-way FaceTime, Anne and Beckett were both super excited when I told them about Wilma and the fire tower. They asked a million questions about Thistledew, and Griffin, and Bear, before Anne cautiously asked about my sister's condition. "Amelia's pretty much the same," I told them, trying to sound less scared than I felt. "She still has a lot of healing and physical therapy to do, but the doctors are hopeful, I guess." As soon as I passed along that good-ish news, I quickly changed the subject, since talking about it probably made everyone uncomfortable.

While my life had taken a massive detour, my friends were planning for their usual summers: packing up to go to summer camp or relatives in Ohio, or training for summer soccer season. Beckett was the only one of my friends willing to admit that he'd biked past my house, and he was also the only one brave enough to tell me what it looked like. My parents had been pretty cagey with details of what was left standing, and I needed to know the truth. "From the front," he said slowly, "it looks pretty much the same. But if you go around back—which I did, because I was curious—it's totally charred. Just a burned shell."

Charred.

Burned shell.

Not words one wanted to hear in relation to her home. My parents still hadn't said anything about what they'd learned about the cause of the fire, and I hadn't asked. I knew I was a coward for not bringing it up, but every time I was going to approach the subject, my parents both looked so weary and sad that I couldn't bring myself to do it. To tell them I was the one to blame.

"The walls in Amelia's bedroom and your bedroom are completely gone, and the windows are all busted out in your dad's office," Beckett said. He stuck his pinkie finger in the corner of his mouth and chewed at his nail—a nervous habit he'd never cracked, even though it often started to bleed. "This morning, a few big machines rolled into your backyard and it kinda looks like they're going to start demolishing it or something."

"Oh, wow. Already?" I said, acting like this wasn't new news. My friends probably thought my parents were keeping me in the loop with everything going on at home, but the reality was, they weren't telling me much of anything. Obviously, they felt like they had to protect me from the facts of our old life. Little did they know that those facts haunted my nightmares, and nothing they did could protect me from reliving that night over and over again in my mind—awake or asleep.

But when I was caring for Wilma or Bear, I could keep myself from getting sucked into a pit of worry. They gave me something important to focus on, so I could forget about the scary what-ifs and my sickening guilt and terrible memories, at least for a little while. Wilma had already gained some weight, and her ribs didn't protrude the way they did when she was a newborn. She was up and about more during the day now, so we let her roam beyond her fenced shed yard, and she and Bear had even started to play together sometimes. Bear would nose her to get her attention, and then Wilma would prance after him as he ran across the yard. She still looked awkward, all long limbs and scrawny body, but she had plenty of energy and loved to get into mischief with Grandpa's garden.

Griffin had decided to research deer for his Cub Scout Critter Care badge. At first, he'd been researching dogs, since he could practice what he learned on Bear (and Bear was really his only option for a pet, since Wendy had already said no to turtles, fish, lizards, cats, and potbellied pigs). But as soon as Wilma showed up on the scene, Griffin had immediately changed course and set to work learning everything he could about raising a healthy fawn.

So, while Grandpa, Bear, and I continued our daily tradition of going out to work at the fire tower, Griffin expertly handled Wilma's day-to-day needs. He had also set up meetings and interviews with the vet who'd checked Wilma over, and a few of the wildlife people at the DNR, to ensure he knew everything there was to know about deer care. And then he took things a step further, by researching wolves, foxes, bears, and raptors—prompting Wendy to tell him, in no uncertain terms, that there would be no more wildlife babies permitted on the premises.

It still hadn't rained for more than a few minutes at a stretch over the past couple of weeks, and Grandpa Howard told me it was very dry all over the upper Midwest. "Dry weather helps fire spread quickly," he told me one morning when we got to the base of the tower. Since the leaves hadn't fully emerged on the trees, he explained, if lightning were to hit a tree or someone's campfire got out of control, it would be very easy for the fire to spread to all the surrounding underbrush. "Dry conditions like these make early spotting really important, so if there *is* a fire that starts, we can catch it and contain it right away."

Later that week, when we were out at the tower, Grandpa actually got to call in some smoke from the little radio he had at the top of the tower. He raced down the stairs to the third landing—where Bear and I had set up shop for the day— buzzing with excitement. He told me the people working back at the Forest Service headquarters had thanked him for the intel and promised they would send someone out to check on it.

"Do they send a fire truck?" I asked him after he

confirmed that it was sufficiently far enough away from us. "Do forest fires work like house fires?"

"First, they usually just send out a crew in a regular car or truck to assess the situation," he said, talking animatedly, clearly somewhat excited about the prospect of spotting a fire. "And then, depending on how big the fire is, what the wind conditions are like, what the surrounding environment looks like—if there's a lot of fuel, like wood and grass and such, in the fire's path—then they'll determine how to handle it."

"*Then* do they send a fire truck?" I asked.

Grandpa laughed. "Some fires are fought by crews on the ground, but it's not like they squirt hoses of water, the way you might expect. Mostly, it's about containing the fire and not letting it spread beyond a certain point. Wildland firefighters will dig trenches and set up a perimeter, trying to stop the fire with a sort of wall. But a lot of fires are fought by plane—they douse the area with a special material that helps suppress the burn."

This was interesting and strange to think about. A house fire was contained; it wasn't often that the fire blazed so big that it spread to neighboring houses, so a fire crew knew the limits of the battle they were fighting. But a forest fire didn't have boundaries and walls and a natural way of stopping it from spreading forever and ever and ever. "Do they ever *not* stop the fire?" I asked, thinking about my nightmares, where the fire often just burned on and on, with no end in sight.

"I'm sure you've heard about all of those fires out west, in

California and Colorado and Utah. And of course, you know about all those bushfires they had to deal with in Australia?" Grandpa said. I nodded. "Those fires can burn for months, sometimes. Dry conditions and big winds can make it tough to get them under control. And with the planet heating up the way it is, fires are going to become more common."

We'd talked about fires out in the western United States and in Australia in school—but those fires had seemed so far away, like they were happening in another world. This tower, Grandpa's perch, was set up to watch for fires *here*, in this world. Even as I considered that, I knew I couldn't—shouldn't—worry about that happening.

That day, Grandpa pointed out the smoke he'd seen crawling up out of the trees a few miles away. When we returned to town that afternoon, we found out it was someone's backyard brush fire that had gotten a little too big. They were able to contain it before it spread past the property line, and I could tell Grandpa felt pretty proud that he'd had a hand in keeping that fire from getting out of control. It was fun to see Grandpa Howard light up and get chatty when the subject came around to something he so obviously cared about. I guess it was like me with Amelia, and Bear, and Wilma, and Griffin—*they* were the things I most cared about. Just like Grandpa with his fire tower and the forest, keeping watch over them made me feel a little stronger. Loving them and protecting them gave me a kind of purpose, I guess.

Later that week, Griffin and I started to work on his next badge: Bear Picnic Basket. For him to earn this badge, we got to create a cookbook full of recipes we could prepare on our own, plan a meal or snack for others, and then cook it— either at home or outdoors.

"I have a very good idea," Griffin told me while we were on our way home from swimming lessons the next Thursday night. We had continued to show up for all our lessons, but we were both progressing slowly. Evan had just been working with us on simple things, like elementary backstroke and treading water. He was trying to get us comfortable in the water so that if we ever found ourselves in a water emergency, we'd have some skills we could use to help us float while we waited for help to arrive. We were all very slowly working up to learning front crawl, at which point Evan had told us he was hoping we'd be ready to put our faces in the water. But every time I tried to float with my face looking down into that murky brown water, thinking of what might be lurking beneath me, I choked and flailed and stood right back up again. At least I knew that I *could* float now. That was a start. Now I just needed to develop a bit of elegance in the water. And because I knew Griffin was watching and taking cues from me, I tried to keep my true emotions and fears from peeking out. *Me* freaking out wasn't going to keep *him* from freaking out.

"What's your very good idea?" I asked Griffin.

"You know how for the Bear Picnic Basket badge, we get to plan a meal, and the Scout book says we can cook a meal for someone either inside *or* outside?"

"Yeah . . ."

"Let's make our meal outside."

"Like, over a campfire?" I asked, feeling my stomach flip.

Griffin grinned. "Wouldn't that be fun? And I was *also* thinking . . . what if we did a campout as part of it? Like, spend the night in a tent and stuff."

"Oh," I said, wishing that sounded like something I would like to do. But it did not. "Where would we camp out? In the backyard?"

"I mean, sure, that's one option," Griffin said. "Or I was sort of thinking we could go on a *real* camping trip. In the woods. I'm supposed to do that sometimes, as part of my Scouting. Camp out. That's something we do. And since *you're* being a Scout *with* me this summer, I thought maybe we could go camping together. Like our own little den, just you and me. And Bear, obviously."

Before I had a chance to talk him out of it, Griffin presented the idea to Grandma Bea, who thought it was a wonderful plan. She began gathering up supplies for us right away. Unsurprisingly, the basement was stuffed full of everything a person could need for any sort of camping trip—hiking, canoeing, biking, traveling by car or motorcycle. They had packs, and camp mats, and cookstoves, and a whole set of little plastic plates and silverware and cups that all matched.

Without consulting me at all, it was decided that we would do our campout the very next night. The forecast looked good and Grandpa Howard happily agreed to be our adult in charge. He suggested we set up camp at the fire tower, where we'd have a nice view of the sunrise, and then Bear could come and we wouldn't have to worry about him running off, since he knew the area so well. Griffin was bursting with excitement about getting to come out to the fire tower with us—he'd asked to come along so many times, but Grandpa had told him there wasn't room on the cycle.

Grandpa seemed especially excited about spending his night sleeping up in the tower. I think, if he'd had the choice, he might just move out to the fire tower for the summer. I guess there were people who did that—lived in a fire tower for the whole spring and summer, throughout the entire fire season. There were national forests and parks out west, in Colorado, Grandpa told me, where the land was so vast and remote and mountainous that human-staffed fire towers hadn't yet been replaced by airplanes and satellite surveillance and drones. I couldn't imagine a worse way to spend my summer, all alone in the middle of the wilderness, just waiting for tragedy to strike. But Grandpa, he seemed like the kind of person who'd been born for that job.

The next day, Griffin and I spent all morning planning a meal we could prepare out on the trail. We'd decided to make pizza dough, and then we could cook it and melt the cheese over the fire—Camp Pizza, Griffin called it. We had also packed up stuff for s'mores, and we were going to cut up carrots and potatoes and onions and roast the mixture with butter in little foil pouches nestled right into the fire. Grandma told me that had been one of Mom's favorite foods growing up. This piece of information seemed crazy to me, since Mom had never made anything like it at home. It was fun hearing about the forgotten parts of my mom's life. She didn't talk much about growing up in Thistledew, so it was kind of nice for me to spend this time getting a peek at what her childhood might have been like. Mom and I were always pretty close, until the fire, and living a version of her childhood helped me feel like I was still a little connected to her here, even when we were physically so far apart.

I was super worried about starting a campfire, but Grandpa assured me that a fire in a firepit, nestled safely at the center of that big rock at the base of the tower, was perfectly safe and nothing I need worry about. There were no tree branches hanging over the area, and no grass grew out of the giant slab of rock. I knew I couldn't let the smell and sight of fire trigger my anxiety forever, so I decided that this would be a good time to try to conquer the fear.

As soon as Grandpa returned from his afternoon shift out at the fire tower, Grandma helped us load all our camping and cookout stuff into the Buick. Then Grandpa got behind the wheel, looking awkward and out of place in the big car, and drove us back out there. At the trail, Griffin bounded out of the car and loaded himself down with packs—one on his front, another on his back. Grandpa carried the bag with the tent, food, water bottles, and cooking gear. I took the big bag full of sleeping bags, which was large but nice and light. I expected Griffin to complain and ask to trade packs halfway up the trail, but he didn't make a peep. Even Bear had a little pack strapped around his chest, with his dog food and a fold-up water dish.

When we reached the base of the tower, Griffin raced up the stairs. He stopped on each stair landing, oohing and aahing at the view. "Come on, Maia!" he cried out. "Come up with me."

"I'll set up the tent," I called back. "You can explore." Grandpa gave me a look. "What?" I snapped. "I haven't told him I don't climb up the tower. He doesn't need to know."

Grandpa shrugged. "Fair enough."

I could hear Griffin shrieking about stuff he could see from way up at the top of the tower. I looked up in time to see his head pop out of one of the little slide-open windows that kept the lookout protected from the elements. My stomach curled just *thinking* about putting my head out a window that high up. "Hey, Maia!" he hollered. "There's Spam up here! Unlimited Spam! You did not tell me about the Spam."

"What did he say?" I asked Grandpa, who was shaking out the tarp that he insisted we put under the tent, just in case it rained in the night. "Did he say there's *Spam* in the tower? Like, the canned-loaves-of-meat stuff? *That* Spam?"

"Yep," Grandpa grunted, and handed me a couple of expandable tentpoles. I fiddled with them, looking over the assembly instruction pictures on the side of the tent bag, trying to figure out where they were supposed to go.

"How much Spam?" I asked, grinning. "Did he say *unlimited* Spam? How much Spam, exactly, would make him think it's unlimited?"

Grandpa glared at me. "I've got a few hundred cans up there, probably."

I dropped the tentpoles. "A few *hundred*? Cans of Spam?" For the first time all summer, I actually felt a tiny urge to climb up all those stairs, just to see this with my own eyes. "Why?"

"Never know when you're gonna need it," he said. "It don't go bad. And I like the taste of it."

"No one likes Spam," I said. "It's an international joke food."

"I like it," Grandpa said. "And *I'm* someone. They wouldn't make it if people didn't eat it. So I guess that makes you wrong."

I laughed. "I guess so."

Grandpa and I finished putting the tent up while Griffin raced around and explored the area around the base of the tower. Bear galloped after him, wherever he went. After we got the tent set up and Griffin organized our stuff inside to make it nice and comfy, Grandpa asked me if I wanted to light the bonfire.

"No," I said, shaking my head vigorously.

"If you're the one controlling it," Grandpa pointed out, "might make it easier for you to be around it."

Griffin nodded his agreement. "I can teach you how to get it started, if you want," he offered. "We learn how to build a good campfire in Scouts."

I considered this. Grandpa had a point—if I knew I was in control, maybe I'd be less afraid. Kind of like caring for

Wilma and floating beside Griffin in the water during our lessons—knowing I had some power over what might happen, and focusing on keeping someone *else* safe, gave me less time to feel afraid. "Yeah," I said. "Okay."

Together, Griffin and I set off to gather twigs and bark to use as kindling and fire starter, as well as some larger chunks of wood to keep the fire going. "Only take wood that's already dead and down," Grandpa told us. "Don't take anything off any of the trees. There's plenty of fuel on the ground, so we don't need to cut any live trees to make our fire."

By the time I began to set up our campfire inside the makeshift stone firepit, we had a pretty impressive stack of wood gathered; enough to keep the fire burning until bedtime and beyond, probably. Griffin showed me how to best stack the wood and kindling so it would catch and take. Then Grandpa helped me light the match, and we gently nestled it into the center of the wood and kindling. At first, there was just a small orange flame—nothing more than an ember. I stared, mesmerized, as that tiny flame caught hold of a piece of dry birch bark, almost instantly flaring up into something much more powerful. I held my breath as the fire crawled onto a larger piece of wood, growing more and more as it consumed the fuel we'd laid out for it.

I took one careful breath at a time, reminding myself that this fire was completely in my control. It wasn't something to fear. But still, as I saw the flickering flames reflected in Griffin's eyes, the memory of that night with Amelia chewed at my memory. Every time I thought of the fire, I couldn't help but think of all we'd lost that night—my sister's skin, our house, the trust that our home was safe and comfortable and would keep us protected from the scary world outside. But now I could also remember how much *hadn't* been destroyed in the fire that night—our lives, our love for each other, and the hope and possibility that things could get better.

With my parents focused on my sister and our house, and my sister's body focused on healing, this summer I was the only one focusing on me. My family had given me the space I needed to heal, and I was fully aware that I needed to use that time to grow. I had felt a wish developing and building during the weeks I'd been in Thistledew, but that night, as I stared into that fire I'd built, I felt the wish flare up and morph into something uncontrollable.

Sitting around the campfire with Grandpa and Griffin and Bear, I felt something in me ignite: an even greater desire to emerge from this summer a stronger version of myself. It wasn't that the old me was *bad*, I kept trying to remind myself, but I now had the chance to build and grow into something more. I'd been wishing all summer that I could change, but that wish no longer felt like enough. I stared into the fire and released my wish, letting it flare up into a promise.

CHAPTER SEVENTEEN

We sat around the fire for hours that night, eating our food as it became ready (the potatoes and carrots took over two hours before they were cooked through, and the Camp Pizza ended up being more pizza-sauce-flavored lumps of scorched dough than actual pizza). Grandpa let us eat s'mores first, explaining, "Your stomach doesn't know what order the food comes in."

To pass the time, Griffin and I sang songs, Bear snoozed and kept watch for intruders who might sneak past the dark shadows beyond the glowing orange circle of the fire, and Grandpa taught us both how to whittle sticks with a little pocketknife he'd brought along. In the fading glow of twilight, he also started teaching us to use a compass, explaining how you can read the numbers and funny wiggling line to track a course through the forest.

"Sometimes," he told us, "I'll spot a smoke from up in the tower that looks like it's not too far away. I'll radio it in from up in the lookout, but then I like to hike out to check on things myself."

"Don't you get scared?" Griffin asked, echoing my thoughts exactly. "What if you *find* the fire . . . then what?"

"Then I'd know its exact location," he said. "And I'd know how big it is, which would give us some sense of what we're dealing with."

"Has that ever happened?" I asked. "Where you actually

walk up to a *live* forest fire?" Grandpa didn't carry a cell phone (and I'd learned from experience that there wasn't any service out here in the middle of the forest anyway), so I wondered what he'd do in that situation. It's not like he could call for help.

"No," he said. "I wouldn't ever get that close to a true fire. That's for the Forest Service to handle. They have plenty of people who are trained to deal with wildland fire. If I were to spot a smoke nearby, it's likely a brand-new fire—in the pre-ignition stage. That's the first stage of a fire, where heat and oxygen combine and start to catch. Oftentimes, a new smoke is just a small fire that will go out on its own—or it's little enough that the Forest Service can deal with it before it gets to the flaming or flashover stage."

Griffin and I exchanged a look. I wasn't about to say this aloud, but I personally didn't think Grandpa's method of searching for forest fires sounded like the way things were supposed to be done.

"I want to fight forest fires," Griffin said.

"You could do that," Grandpa told him. "When you're older. They're always looking for people who are strong, brave, and good at working with a team to help out with fire efforts."

"Have you ever fought a forest fire?" I asked, wondering why I'd never thought to ask that before. Grandpa Howard was brave, and tough, and it seemed like the kind of thing he'd want to do. I guess it was that Grandpa just seemed so *old*. It felt weird to think of him ever being young and wild.

Grandpa shook his head. "No, I never got the chance." Then he wandered off, heading toward the edge of the trees. He was obviously done talking about it for the night.

It felt like midnight by the time Griffin and I climbed into our tent, but when we checked Griffin's watch, it was only nine. It's just that it was so dark outside, and once the fire had been put out—we'd doused it with gallons and gallons of water, to make sure no stray embers crept out of the fire bed and created problems in the night—I wanted to go to sleep. Grandpa climbed up the stairs to the tower, where he was sleeping that night, and Griffin and I retreated to our sleeping bags inside the tent.

The wind blew whisper-soft in the trees just outside the thin fabric of our tent, and I could hear Bear shifting to get comfortable in the spot he'd picked as his bed for the night. Somewhere far off, a lone wolf howled out a solemn cry. "Hey, Maia?" Griffin whispered, several long minutes after we'd both tucked in for the night.

"Yeah?"

"How come you won't go up the tower?" he asked. "Are you afraid of heights?"

I flipped onto my back, staring up at the shadows of branches making patterns on the roof of the tent. "Why do you ask?"

"You didn't come up to show me around the tower before, and I think we can both agree that inside the watchtower would be a much cooler spot to camp tonight. But instead, we're sleeping down here on the ground in this tent while your grandpa sleeps up there alone."

"Oh," I said. "Yeah, I guess the tower probably would be a pretty cool place to have a campout," I agreed. "But this tent is cool, too."

For once, Griffin didn't respond.

"I've always been afraid of heights," I reluctantly told him. "And drowning, and falling, and now fire. I'm a little bit afraid of everything, I guess." But what I'd been realizing was, my fears always felt a little *less* lately, especially when someone else—Griffin, or Grandpa, or Wilma—needed me to be strong for them. I hadn't had that strength the night of the fire, but since then, I couldn't imagine ever letting someone down that badly again.

"Me too," Griffin said. I could hear the rustle of his sleeping bag as he rolled to face me in the dark. "I'm scared of lots of things. That's normal, right?"

I considered this. "Yeah," I said. "It's normal to be afraid of things."

"But it gets better as I get older, right?" he asked softly.

"Sometimes," I told him, not wanting to tell him that a lot of times, your fears grow with you. Mine had.

Griffin's breathing leveled out beside me, and I could tell he was close to falling sleep. Then he muttered, "I guess fears are little bit like a forest fire, then. If you catch them before they get too big, they're easier to keep under control." He sighed and rolled to face the other way. "Good night, Maia. Sweet dreams."

• • •

That night, there were no nightmares. I don't know if I slept peacefully because my sleeping bag hugged me tight inside the cozy tent, or because of the background chorus of nature that blanketed us as we slept, or because of Griffin's soft breathing beside me that sounded so much like my sister's. Whatever it was, I was happy to wake up with no terrible visions chasing me into the day.

After we packed up the tent, we made cold, deconstructed s'mores for breakfast—a plain graham cracker, a couple of raw marshmallows, and a bar of chocolate each. Griffin and I hadn't planned a breakfast, and none of us wanted to start a fire, but we also didn't have the energy to set off down the trail to the car without eating something.

When we got home, Bear was the first one out of the car. He trotted across the yard to greet Wilma, who was relaxing and snacking in her little pen. It looked like she'd gotten bigger in the past twenty-four hours. Our little fawn was growing stronger every day, and her appetite just kept growing with her. She'd started munching on grass in the yard, and she had developed quite a temper when her bottle wasn't ready exactly when she wanted it.

As hard as it was to think about ever letting her go, Grandma and I had started looking into wildlife education centers where Wilma could go to live after she'd gotten so big that Grandma and Grandpa's yard wasn't enough for her any longer. None of us wanted her to wander out into the woods that surrounded town on all sides, since she'd been raised without ever having to fend for or feed herself. And frankly, with Bear always nearby to protect her, she probably didn't have any of the necessary skills for survival out in the wild. Griffin and I both loved the idea of Wilma living in a deer preserve, where people could watch and learn from her, and where she'd be protected from the scary life she'd face if she were released out into the woods on her own.

That afternoon, after I called home to check on my sister and parents, Griffin and I got started on Griffin's Marble Madness badge. Grandma Bea offered to teach us how to play a marble game, while also telling us about the history of marbles. I'd always thought they were just pretty glass balls that you collected and maybe filled vases with, but it turned out there were all kinds of games you could play with them.

After playing marbles with Grandma for a while, Griffin wanted to set up a marble racecourse. We tried making a maze in Grandma and Grandpa's backyard, but Wilma kept knocking over everything we set up—she liked to nose at the colorful marbles. So we moved our project to Griffin's fort and built a cardboard marble maze that wound all the way from the snack space to his nap nest.

Summer in Thistledew had finally eased into a comfortable routine. We were marching along on Griffin's badge work, Bear was a well-behaved student, Wilma was thriving, and both Griffin and I were starting to make serious progress at swimming lessons. With our teacher Evan bobbing along beside us, we each actually managed to swim a few strokes of front crawl with our faces in the water that week. Griffin and I were the only two in our lesson group who had (so far) managed to swim all the way out to the buoys at the far edge of the swimming area. He told us it was looking like we'd probably be ready to earn our trip out to the inflatable slide and climbing wall on the last day!

One day after class, Evan took me aside and said I might want to consider joining the older, advanced group when they took their victory swim out to the wooden raft in a few weeks. For one split second, I started to shake my head no, thinking that an impossibility. But then I remembered my promise to try to push myself to be a new kind of person; to stop letting fears hold me back. So even though the idea of swimming out to that wooden raft terrified me, I smiled at Evan and said, "Maybe. But let's get Griff out to the bouncy slide first, okay?"

Everything was finally beginning to click into place, which meant I wasn't at all prepared when my parents called with bad news. Amelia had developed an infection after her latest skin grafting surgery, and she wasn't doing well. They couldn't keep her fever down and she wasn't responding to treatments. For the first time since I'd gotten to Thistledew, the possibility was really and truly out there: I might never see my sister again.

Still, as the visions forced their way back in, I didn't ask about coming home. I already knew the answer: It wasn't time.

That's not what my family needed from me right now, and I was finally ready to admit that I wasn't able to be there for them yet, either. When it was time, I felt sure I would know. And when the time came, I would be ready.

CHAPTER EIGHTEEN

Grandma must have talked to Mom and gotten the latest on my sister, because she spent the rest of Friday night and all day Saturday keeping me extra busy with Wilma. I guess it was good she did, since focusing on something else helped me stop obsessing about Amelia's fever.

But this time, it didn't make me forget. Because I was terrified.

What if my sister didn't pull through this new challenge? What if she *never* got better?

I tried to replay Grandpa's words in my head. These were things I couldn't control. Worrying endlessly about the future wouldn't help anyone. But what I could help in that moment was Wilma, so I decided to focus all my energy on cleaning out her hay, fixing pieces of fencing that had gotten wonky, and even sweeping and clearing out all the stuff off the middle shelves in the shed. Now that she was getting bigger and more curious about *everything*, we were trying to keep things out of her reach. I finished all my tasks (with some help from Griffin, who had basically half moved in to Wilma's shed) by late Saturday, and spent that night sleeping fitfully through nightmare after nightmare.

It was nearly impossible to fall asleep, since I knew that as soon as I did, the terrorizing images would return. The scenes in my dreams had grown and morphed into something all-consuming. Sometimes Wilma, Bear, or Griffin made a guest appearance in my nighttime fires. Grandma must have expected that night would be bad, because when I woke up on Sunday morning she was perched at the kitchen table, already fully dressed, with a giant map spread out on the table before her. "Good morning," she said, offering me a weak smile. "We're skipping church again because I have a special trip planned for us today."

I'd learned to enjoy the days spent with Grandpa out at the fire tower, but a day with Grandma Bea was an extra-special treat. She always planned something new for us to do together, and so far, she hadn't struck out with a single one of her ideas. Still, the last thing I wanted to do was have a fun adventure while my sister fought for her life.

I was grateful to her for trying to take my mind off Amelia's pain, though, even when I knew nothing could make me forget what my sister was going through back home. I hoped that staying busy would keep me from twisting myself into a helpless knot of guilt and sadness. And being so far away, I knew there was nothing I could do for her beyond keeping Mom and Dad from worrying about me, too. "Where are we going?"

"I'm going to take you out to the pictographs on Hegman Lake."

"What's that?"

"An ancient generation of Native Americans—historians are pretty sure it was an Indigenous Ojibwe tribe, but no one knows for sure—painted pictures on some large rocks out in the Boundary Waters. It's an impressive piece of history from around these parts that I want to share with you." She stood up and went to the stove, turning on a burner. "Get dressed for a day on the lake, and I'll make you some eggs."

When I dug through my stuff to find something good to wear on our canoe trip, I found Beckett's favorite soccer jersey stuffed deep down at the very bottom of my pile of borrowed shirts. I brought it to my face and breathed in the comforting scent of home and friends, and decided it was the perfect thing. Instead of making me sad and lonely, like it had when I'd first left Chicago, putting it on now made me think about everything and everyone waiting for me at home when it was time for me to go back.

After I was dressed and had eaten, Grandma and I worked together to carry a big canoe from behind the house and strap it on top of the car. Bear bounded around, keeping himself annoyingly underfoot, obviously hoping he wouldn't be forgotten on this outing. "Can he come?" I asked Grandma. I needed him more than ever today.

"How do you think he'll do in a canoe?" she asked me. "If he moves around a lot, we're all gonna go over."

I stared into Bear's eyes. He stared back seriously, unblinking. "Can you handle yourself in a canoe, big guy?" He cocked his head, wagged his tail, and gave me one of his lopsided smiles. I laughed, then said to Grandma, "I guess the worst thing that happens is we all get wet."

Grandma tossed a couple of life jackets in the back of the

car, and even managed to rustle up an old dog life jacket from somewhere deep in their creepy basement. I knew Bear could swim, since I'd seen him romp and play and dive after sticks in the water out at the other end of the beach during my and Griffin's swimming lessons, but a life jacket for everyone certainly made me feel more comfortable—especially if we might tip. Once we'd loaded the trunk up with a lunch, some paddles, and a couple of towels ("just in case," Grandma said), we hit the road.

To get to the pictographs, we had to drive down a long, winding paved road and park the car in a little gravel parking lot. There were a few other cars and trucks there, but no people that I could see. Grandma filled out a form—a day-use permit to visit the Boundary Waters for the day, she said—and tucked it into a little wooden box hanging near the big map at the start of the trail.

While I unloaded Bear and the gear from the trunk, Grandma somehow got the canoe off the car and onto her shoulders. She made it look so easy—with only a few loud grunts and one bad word that told me it *wasn't* actually easy—and somehow slid that big, long boat off the car and onto her shoulders, where she balanced it in midair. With the canoe settled, and the life jackets dangling casually off her strong arms, Grandma Bea set off down a trail to the lake. I quickly grabbed one paddle in each hand and the rest of our stuff, and Bear and I chased after her.

"We have to walk across this short portage to get to the lake," Grandma called out to me from beneath the turtle shell of canoe on her back. Before this summer, I'd had no idea what a portage was. Now I knew that it was a path where people could carry their boats to or between lakes that you couldn't drive to. Her voice echoed as she said, "There aren't any motorized vehicles allowed in most of the Boundary Waters—only canoes."

The portage was well-worn and bumpy, but it wasn't nearly as long as the walk up to the fire tower. It was just a little trickier navigating this trail with a full lunch pack on my back and a canoe paddle in each hand—they kept bumping on rocks and trees as I navigated corners and hills. Grandma told me that some people camped out in the Boundary Waters for weeks or even months at a time. "To get away from everything," she explained. "They pack in food, supplies, and whatever else they need to survive off the grid for a while."

I couldn't imagine carrying enough stuff on my back to survive for more than a few days. But then again, I hadn't been able to imagine surviving a few days, let alone weeks, in Thistledew when I'd first arrived. I guess anyone who chose this kind of journey was prepared to do whatever it took to figure it out.

The wind was blowing hard when we emerged from the trail at the edge of the lake, so Grandma steered our canoe close to shore. This meant we would have to paddle farther to reach our destination, she said, rather than cutting straight across the middle. But she promised the longer, calmer route would be easier than trying to battle the wind.

She also explained that, with Bear on board, we were a little unsteady—and it was easier to deal with a tip-over when you weren't in the middle of the lake.

There was a short "lift-over portage," as Grandma called it, between South Hegman Lake and North Hegman. Once we had all our stuff and ourselves loaded back in the canoe, we paddled together past islands and through sections of the lake where there was grass growing up out of the water. "Did you know wild rice grows in water like this?" Grandma asked me. "Back when your mom was little, your grandfather and I used to go out together and pick it instead of buying it at the store like I do these days. He'd paddle, and I'd sit in the middle of the canoe and beat the rice right into the bottom of the boat."

"Rice *grows* in water?" I asked.

Grandma laughed. I guess that was my answer.

Soon, we came upon these huge slabs of rock that were jutting straight out of the water. The edge of the lake was lined with cliffs of rock that looked like they had been sliced off a massive stone mountain at some point in history. Grandma steered the canoe right up near the rock's face, and suddenly, she pointed. "There's one of the rock paintings," she told me. I followed her finger and saw a faded, rust-colored shape that I guessed was one of the pictographs we'd come out here to see. I couldn't tell what it was, but then Grandma pointed to another and I started to notice shapes in the colors. One looked like a fish, another like a deer or moose or something. "Do they mean something?" I asked.

"It's impossible for anyone to know for sure," Grandma said. "Some people think the drawings were probably meant to be spiritual, or retellings of critical moments in history." We floated past the rock face, and I kept a close look out for more pictures, trying to make sense of them. They were all pretty faded and difficult to see too clearly because the paint—whatever those original artists had used to draw them—had been exposed to elements for hundreds and hundreds of years. It was amazing they'd survived at all. I thought about that—how cool it would be for your story to live on, to share with people hundreds of years in the future.

Grandma went on, "Some other folks, they think maybe the pictographs are meant to be re-creations of legends or hunting stories from ancient Native American tribes. Another group of historians think maybe there's some connection between the pictures and celestial events." She paddled on. "No one really knows for sure, so I suppose you can take your own guess. But no matter what their original purpose was, it's really neat to know that this is someone's story, saved here on these rocks for all this time."

We floated on in silence, making our way around the edge of the lake. Through the trees, I spotted a pair of deer staring silently back at me, still as one of the enormous tree trunks that flanked them on all sides. Luckily, Bear didn't see them, or I have a feeling he'd have barked and startled them, or run to greet them, thinking it was

Wilma's long-lost family. Maybe it was; maybe this was Wilma's aunt and uncle, here to say hello. It was fun to think about.

When we spotted an island with a big, bald, rocky spot sticking out on one end of it, Grandma and I paddled toward it. She eased the canoe up against the shore so we could get out and eat our lunch. Bear was excited to pee on a few new trees and shrubs, and immediately set off to sniff around. After we ate, Grandma suggested we go swimming in our clothes off the island. "If you get into your life jacket upside down," she told me, demonstrating as she stepped into the armholes and shimmied the vest up her body, "it looks kinda like a diaper. You can float in the water without your arms feeling trapped. Your mom used to like swimming like this. She'd bob around out in the lake all day."

I liked thinking about my mom doing some of these same things when she was my age. Maybe that was why she'd decided to send me here, to Thistledew. Even though *she'd* left "The End of the Road" for the big city, I bet she still remembered how comforting all this clean air and nature out here could be. I imagined so.

Grandma waded into the dark, unfamiliar lake, wearing her shorts and tank top under that big, puffy floating diaper. Sandals on, she walked gingerly into the reddish water, stepping carefully over slick, mossy rocks, and finally eased her body into the depths. "Ahh," she sighed. Bear tried to slip in after her, but found it was too hard for his paws to get past the lumpy rocks to enter the lake. He sat, perched like a little watchdog, onshore. "Come on in, Maia. It's nice and warm."

Without giving myself a chance to chicken out, I eased into my life jacket diaper and waded out to meet Grandma. The water dropped off very suddenly, and in a single step, I was in over my head. For a moment, my head slipped under, but then my floating diaper lifted me back up and I was bobbing, suspended, in the middle of a lake.

"Feels good, doesn't it?" Grandma said with a smile. She leaned back, resting her head in the water. I followed suit. The diaper acted like a sort of recliner, letting me relax while supporting me at the same time. It was so calming that I didn't even care about what might be swimming by underneath me. We just floated together like that for what felt like hours, staring up at the sky. Wisps of clouds drifted overhead, but otherwise the sky was a perfect, pearly blue.

I hadn't realized how far we'd drifted out from the island until Grandma said, "Want to swim all the way to the other shore?" I turned and looked back at the island, which was now much, much farther away than I would normally have felt comfortable with. But after all my swimming lessons, and wearing that floaty diaper, I felt pretty good. Bear had found a comfy spot on the warm rock face at the end of our lunch island, and he appeared to be fast asleep. So, Grandma and I began the slow process of kicking toward the far lakeshore.

"We'll need to swim back still, you know," she reminded me. "So let me know if you're getting tired and want to turn around."

"I know," I said. "I will." But I didn't want to give up. I wanted to make it to that far shore. When I started to get tired of my messy dog paddle, I flipped onto my back and kicked, eyes trained up at the sky. With my head back in the water, my ears were submerged, and the whole world disappeared into muffled background noise. I don't know how Grandma could have guessed that this was just what I needed today, but now that we were out here, I knew this getaway from the real world was exactly the right medicine.

When we were close to shore, I reached my foot down and touched bottom. The rocks underfoot were sort of slimy and slippery, but I managed to find a few spots with just sand and stones where it was easier to get a foothold. Slowly, Grandma and I climbed up onshore and then looked across the water to see how far we'd come. Bear was now sitting on the island, watching us warily, and I waved at him to let him know we were okay.

"Can we take a quick break before we swim back?" I asked.

"Take as long as you like," Grandma said. She sat down in a sunny patch right onshore while I climbed gingerly up the rocky shoreline and stepped into a short crop of trees just a few paces back from the water. Grandma called after me, "Do the trees over here look a little different to you?"

I had just noticed that all the trees in this area were much shorter and smaller than others we'd paddled by that day, and the ground seemed fresher; cleaner, somehow. "Yeah," I said. "They're little. What's the deal?"

"You're standing on the former site of a controlled burn," she told me. "About a dozen years back, this part of the Boundary Waters caught fire during a lightning strike. Rather than putting it out, the Forest Service decided to let the area burn. But now the trees and flowers are finally starting to grow back."

I stepped quickly out of the trees, not wanting to get any closer to the ruins. It was impossible not to think about this forest on fire, consumed by flames that would chew up everything in the path of their destruction.

"Forest fires are a perfectly natural part of the forest," Grandma told me, obviously sensing my unease. But she couldn't possibly have any idea just *how* uneasy I felt, my bare toes touching earth that was once ravaged by fire. "They're an important part of the ecosystem, and they play an important role in keeping the forest healthy. The Forest Service even *prescribes* burns, when conditions are right, and when they know it makes sense to let an area of the wilderness burn for a while."

I could barely hear what she was saying. Suddenly, the only thing I could hear were the flames from that night, the rushing of the air as it was gobbled up by smoke, that terrifying sound of Amelia's curtains catching in the blaze.

Across the lake, Bear barked, a warning.

"We have to go," I choked out, only then realizing that I'd started to cry. My tears mixed with the lake water dripping out of my hair. "I need to leave." My voice got louder. The burned forest was making me think of all that my family had lost in our own fire. "I don't want to be here anymore."

Grandma hugged me tight, squeezing rivulets of water out of both our wet life jackets. "Maia," she whispered right into my ear. "Shush, now. It's okay. The fire is long gone. There's no need for you to be afraid here—"

"It's *not* okay," I sobbed, cutting her off as I shoved away. "Why would they just *let* it burn? What if someone was out here—someone who didn't know the fire had started? What if they were asleep in a tent, and suddenly, the fire overtook them?"

"Maia," Grandma said calmly, now holding my wrist like I was a prisoner. I wanted to bolt, to jump into the lake and get off this fire-ravaged, destroyed patch of land. "That wouldn't happen. Whenever there's a controlled or pre-scribed burn, there are warnings. The area is restricted. Even when a forest fire crops up suddenly out here in the Boundary Waters, they have crews of wilderness rangers who make sure everyone is out."

I stared at her, trying to figure out if she was telling me the truth. She'd never lied to me before, so I had no reason to doubt her. I took a deep breath and nodded, feeling the tears slowing. I sniffed and said, "I still don't understand why they would just let the woods burn. It seems terrible to think that they would just let all those trees and flowers and stuff die."

"Sometimes," Grandma explained, "a forest *needs* to burn to get rid of some of the fuel on the ground. It allows the forest to renew itself. The old wood burns, and that lets new growth in, to help rebuild that part of the forest." She gestured out toward the lake, and I followed her gaze—looking out at the endless wilderness that stretched on for hundreds of miles to our north, all the way up to Canada. While I forced myself not to think about what would happen if that whole forest went up in a mighty blaze, Grandma continued, "A bunch of years back, there were some huge winds that blew through this area, and that storm left a lot of downed trees. All of those dead trees on the ground became a hazard, just waiting to catch fire. This forest needed to burn in order to survive and thrive."

"When they decide to let it burn, how do they keep a fire from spreading too far?" I wondered aloud. "Couldn't it just keep burning for miles and miles?"

"It could, yes," Grandma said. "But usually, the Forest Service is able to build a fire line all around the area, so it won't creep farther than it should. They manage these controlled burns carefully, keeping them well within their control. And they only let a fire keep burning if conditions are in their favor—wind levels, humidity. They suppress it if they think there's any risk of it spreading." She looked at me seriously. "But I'm not going to lie to you: Sometimes, even controlled or planned burns can get out of control when things go wrong. Mother Nature is strong-willed and powerful. Some things, nature especially, are out of our control. And we've got to accept that."

I appreciated Grandma's honesty. She wasn't trying to tell me nothing bad *ever* happened, but she was trying to help me understand how something that seemed so awful could sometimes be a good thing. And even if it wasn't always a *good* thing, it was *survivable*. If even a massive forest could bounce back from devastation and destruction, so could we.

That's when I realized I needed to be honest with her, too. It was time to share the secret that had been burning inside me all summer. Standing atop the buried ashes of that long-forgotten forest fire, I decided it was time for me to open up and spill my secret. "I started the fire the night Amelia got hurt," I said in a voice just louder than a whisper. "I was burning a candle in my room, and I must have forgotten to put it out."

Grandma shook her head and pulled her eyebrows together, obviously not wanting to believe that it was true. Obviously horrified by what I'd done.

"It's true," I said.

"No, Maia," Grandma whispered, her face filled with concern and so many questions.

"It was an accident," I said. "I just forgot about it, I guess. And then Amelia was trapped in her bedroom, without any warning at all. She was just sleeping peacefully, and I almost killed her." I choked out another sob, the tears running down my cheeks again. "I started it, and I was too slow to get her out before the fire caught her, too." Too scared to help her as quickly as I should have.

"Maia," Grandma said, pulling me in for a hug. "Oh, hon, have you been keeping this worry to yourself all summer?"

I nodded into her shoulder.

"Oh, baby girl," she whispered. "Oh, sweetheart."

I let the tears flow, allowed my grandma to hold me and rock me and soothe me in a way I hadn't realized I desperately needed. She didn't shush me, or tell me it would be all right, or tell me I was wrong. She just let me cry and held me tight.

When I was finally all cried out, I pulled back and looked into her face. "I'm sorry," I said.

Grandma sighed. "I'm sorry you've been dealing with that on your own. I had no idea you've been carrying this burden alone."

"Everyone thinks I'm the hero who pulled my sister out of that fire," I said to her, nearly starting to cry again. "But really, I'm the monster who started it."

Grandma shook her head again. "Even if it *was* your candle that started the fire," she told me, "you're not a monster. But you *are* a hero, Maia, because it takes a special kind of love to walk through flames and pull your baby sister to safety." She looked at me sharply. "Most importantly, you can't blame yourself for any of this. So many factors played into what happened that night, and if you hadn't acted when and how you did, who knows what might have happened? You can't second-guess things now." She tsked and said, more to herself than to me, "And we don't even *know* that your candle was to blame. I'm going to get to the bottom of this, do a little digging. It's entirely possible the candle may not have been the thing that caused the fire in the first place. Won't know until we ask."

I nodded. "Thank you." I had been avoiding asking my parents about the fire department's investigation into the cause of the fire because I thought it would hurt too much to know. But as soon as Grandma Bea offered to look into it for me, I realized I might actually feel better if I had the facts. At least then I'd know for sure, and maybe I'd finally be able to start moving past the guilt. "Do you promise to tell me the truth about what you learn?"

"I promise," she vowed. Then she hugged me again and said, "Think you're ready to swim back to Big Bear now? I'm pretty sure the poor dog heard you crying over here. I think he's been trying to find a way off the island and into the water so he could swim over here and be with you for the past five minutes. Let's go save him from his misery, shall we?"

"Let's," I laughed, feeling lighter and more hopeful than I had in a while. "I'll race you."

CHAPTER NINETEEN

"Do you see your brother much?" I asked Grandpa on our hike up to the fire tower the next morning. I'd been thinking about that picture in his camper, the one of Grandpa Howard and his brother as teenagers. They looked like they had been close, maybe even as close as me and Amelia. "Does he live nearby, or did he move away, like Mom? Do you have any other siblings?"

"No other siblings. Doesn't live nearby," Grandpa said. Then, in the same even voice, he said, "James is dead."

"Oh." I wasn't sure what to say to that. Grandpa had delivered this news with so little emotion. "Did he pass away a long time ago?"

"When he was nineteen," Grandpa told me. "I was seventeen when we lost him."

"I'm sorry."

I'd overheard him and Grandma talking through my window last night, talking out by Grandpa's firepit about what I'd confessed to her yesterday. I'd told her she could tell him, since I didn't want to have to be the one who did, and I knew he'd hear it all eventually. "What do you have to be sorry for about James?" Grandpa asked. Now he stopped on the path and turned to face me, squinting in the bright morning sunlight. "It's not your fault he's gone."

I nodded. "I know. It's just, I'm sorry he's dead, I guess. That's really sad." I had imagined, too many times this summer, what it would be like to lose my sister. To suddenly be an only child, when so much of my life was being a big sister.

Grandpa heaved a sigh. Then he picked something out of his teeth and stared me down. "I'm the one who's sorry. He's only dead 'cause of me."

My mouth opened. I didn't know what to say to that. I had a feeling Grandpa wasn't exactly eager to open himself up to questions, but I had to know what had happened. I also had a feeling he'd only brought this up because of what he knew about me and the night of the fire. "Why?"

He sat down on a rock, right there on the edge of the trail. Bear had bounded up ahead of us, but he came sprinting back down the path when he realized we weren't behind him. This wasn't the usual way things were done in the morning—we didn't just *stop* on the way up to the tower—and any change in routine always seemed to make Bear uncomfortable. Also, there were big thunderstorms in the forecast for that afternoon—the first in weeks—and Griffin had told me that some dogs could sense changes in barometric pressure. I guessed Bear was one of these dogs, since he'd been extra fidgety and crazy all morning. "James and I, when we were kids, we split duties up here in the fire tower," Grandpa said. "We took turns keeping watch as our summer job."

I nodded, urging him to keep going.

"I hated the job. But my brother, he loved it. Enjoyed the solitude, loved getting a chance to come up here and read or draw while he kept watch over the forest he loved so much." Grandpa stared off into the trees. I tried not to move, not wanting to break the spell that had gotten my grandpa talking for more than five seconds. "Me, I wasn't a good kid. Got into a lot of trouble, and I didn't always think about how my actions affected other people. Well, one day, it was my turn to keep watch up here. I left home early, like always. But then I took off—went for a drive on my motorcycle and spent the day just doing whatever I felt like doing." He took a deep breath. "Honestly, I don't even remember all of what I did that day—spent some time at the lake, met up with a couple friends to play cards, just drove around taking time for myself. Alls I know is, that's the day a fire started just outside town and there was no one up there to spot the smoke."

I took a quick, sharp breath. Even though I'd had a pretty good sense of where his story was heading, it wasn't easy to hear him say it out loud.

He fixed me with a serious look. "It had been a hot spring, and the forest was dry. Worse yet, the winds that day were really whipping and when that spark caught, it started to spread quickly. I was nowhere nearby when they called up crews to go out and help fight the blaze. A bunch of guys from town all volunteered to help out, and James was one of them. The fire was going strong by the time they got out to the edge of it and started trying to create a line to contain it. My brother was right up front, I guess, always wanting to be a hero."

Grandpa stopped, then reached down to rub Bear's floppy ears.

"He died in a forest fire?" I whispered.

Grandpa shook his head. "Not exactly. They got the fire under control and everything was looking pretty good. By the time I got home that night, thanks to all those volunteers, they had gotten it almost completely contained. It was a miracle they got the blaze under control as quickly as they did. Just a few acres ended up burning."

"So—" I began, needing to understand what had happened. But Grandpa cut me off.

"A group of the younger guys volunteered to stick around after things were under control and do mop-up. That's where they go back through the burn area and make sure there isn't anything left smoldering that might snag and catch fire again later." Grandpa rested his elbows on his knees, staring down at the ground. "There were a couple of trees still standing in that area. They'd been burned real bad and weren't very stable. As the mop-up crew was passing through, one of the trees cracked off halfway up its trunk." I closed my eyes, not wanting to imagine the scene in my head, but unable to avoid it either. Grandpa went on, "It landed on my brother. James died instantly, I guess."

I stood there in silence for a long time, trying to imagine how it must have felt to be Grandpa that day. How it must feel to be Grandpa every day, blaming himself for what had happened.

"If I'd been where I was supposed to be, the story would have ended differently," he said, standing up. He began to hike again, his shoulders slouched under the weight of our lunch pack. Bear trotted beside him, obviously sensing that Grandpa needed him more than I did at the moment.

"It isn't your fault he died," I called after him.

"I know I couldn't have stopped the fire from starting," Grandpa said. "And maybe he still would have been out there fighting it that night. But timing is everything. If I'd called that fire in sooner, who knows what might have happened? A few minutes can change everything."

I understood that—a few minutes *could* change everything. If I'd gone to my sister's room just a few minutes earlier, maybe I could have gotten Amelia out with only minor injuries. If I'd been a few minutes later, she'd be dead. "You can't blame yourself," I said. I needed him to believe it, so I could make myself believe it, too.

"I know that; I really do," he said. "But it can't change how I feel, deep down."

"Is that the reason you come out to the fire tower every day? To make up for what happened fifty years ago?"

"I guess that's part of it," Grandpa said. "And because I like it up here. Because *he* liked it up here. It helps me remember James, and keeps me focused on something worthwhile." By now, we'd reached the top of the trail. The stairs loomed ahead of us; the forest spread out all around us like an emerald ocean.

"Grandpa?" I said as he headed toward the tower steps.

It was time for us to each go our separate ways—me and Bear waiting down on solid ground, while Grandpa Howard kept watch over his world from above. But before he left, I had to say something. I needed to get it off my chest.

"We still don't know if I'm to blame for the fire at our house," I began, stumbling to find the words. Grandma told me she had called Mom as soon as we got back from our canoe trip the previous day, to ask what they knew about the cause of the fire. I guess because our house was so severely damaged, and because the arson investigator was really backlogged, it was taking a long time to release an official cause. It sounded like they suspected faulty wiring, but there was still the possibility it could have been my candle that started the blaze. The fact that I *had* a candle in my room was certainly complicating the investigation.

Even if it wasn't my fault the fire had started, I still felt responsible for everything else that happened that night. I blinked at Grandpa and said, "And maybe it was all my fault, maybe it wasn't . . . But no matter what caused the fire, I *know* it's my fault Amelia didn't get out of the house sooner." I sighed. "So, I guess what I'm saying is, I get how you feel."

He shook his head. "You can't think that, Maia. You shouldn't be blaming yourself at all. So many factors played into what happened at your house that night, and no one thing is to blame—it was a fluke, a horrible, tragic accident. What matters most is you did everything you needed to do to get your sister out of there even when it must have been terrifying for you." He stepped closer to me, still shaking his head. "You saved your sister; you need to understand that."

"If you think what happened to Amelia wasn't my fault, then what happened to James *definitely* wasn't your fault," I argued. "*You* need to see that."

"But I didn't do what I was supposed to do that day. I wasn't up here when I said I would be," Grandpa said, his face a mess of emotions. "You did the right thing that night; you were a hero. I was a coward."

"Grandpa," I said quietly, stepping toward him. Carefully, slowly, I put my arms around him and gave him a hug. I think it was the first time we'd ever hugged, except for when I was on the back of the motorcycle. His shirt was sort of scratchy, but his arms were warm and solid, and he hugged me back. "Grandpa, you'll never know how things would have played out even if you *had* been keeping watch up in the tower that day. That tree still might have fallen; your brother might have died that same day in some other way. You can't ever know for sure. But you have to stop blaming yourself. Promise?" I stepped back and looked right into his eyes. "If you forgive yourself, then maybe I can stop blaming myself, too."

Grandpa took a big breath. Finally, he nodded. "I can try."

"That's good enough," I said. I looped my arm through his, and we stood there for a while, high above everything.

I had a feeling both of us were probably thinking about the way things could have been and wishing our tragedies had played out a different way. But I really hoped that now we might both be able to move on and accept what had happened, instead of trying to rewrite the past.

CHAPTER TWENTY

By the time Grandpa Howard came down from the tower for lunch, the wind at the top of our rocky hill had begun to whip and whistle through the trees that surrounded us. The storm clouds that spent most of the morning lurking on the horizon had crept closer, and the sky overhead was growing increasingly dark as afternoon set in. It almost looked like Amelia's favorite tie-dyed T-shirt, colored in swirls of green and dark blue and purple.

"Do we need to hike out of here?" I asked, watching Grandpa casually munch on his BLT. He didn't seem particularly worried about the weather. But truth be told, he didn't ever seem particularly worried about much of anything. "I mean, it feels like a tall metal tower on the peak of a hill isn't the safest place to ride out a storm."

"The tower's grounded," Grandpa grunted. "If lightning struck, the current would course right through and get buried deep in the ground. We'd feel a tingle, maybe, or even see our hair stand on end. But it's not as if a shot of lightning would kill us if it hit the tower. There's nothing to worry about."

"Um," I said, pointing to myself. "What about someone who's not actually *on* the fire tower? Like, say, me? And Bear?"

"Sit up on the first stair landing with the dog," Grandpa told me. "You've gone that high enough times by now; it shouldn't be too tough for you to climb partway up today. That way you'll be protected from the rain if it starts pouring *and* you won't get electrocuted if lightning hits somewhere on the top of the hill." He winked. "Sound like a plan?"

"Yep," I squeaked. "There's nothing quite like someone mentioning words like 'pouring' and 'electrocuted' to make a girl feel comfy and confident."

Grandpa nodded, obviously not sensing my sarcasm. "Great."

As soon as we'd packed up our lunch remains, Grandpa stood to head back up to the top of the tower. "These are exactly the right conditions for a fire to start," he explained as he climbed alongside me, up to that first stair landing. "The forest is brittle and dry from lack of rain, the leaf cover on the trees is still minimal, winds are stiff, and this looks like the kinda storm that could produce cloud-to-ground lightning. Now would be a pretty stinkin' bad time for us to leave this tower."

I tried to look at it from Grandpa Howard's perspective. He felt it was his lifelong duty to sit up in this tower, protecting the town from any future fires. He'd carried the guilt of his brother's death for more than fifty years, and that guilt had tied him to this post forever. I could see why he'd be reluctant to leave now, in perfect forest fire conditions. But that didn't necessarily make *me* any more excited about sitting out in the middle of the woods in the middle of a storm, literally waiting for lightning to strike. Sure, I'd learned to manage some of my worries a *bit* this summer, but this whole scenario was more than I was prepared to handle.

For the next hour or so, Bear and I crouched together on that tower landing, watching as the clouds stirred and bubbled and grew like rising bread dough all across the sky. From this vantage point, so high up, it really was pretty magnificent to watch Mother Nature do her work. A few of the clouds were stuffed with lightning, and they glowed and pulsed with energy as the storm crackled and buzzed within, struggling to burst out and explode in streaks of golden heat.

Far, far off I could hear the faint rumble of thunder as the storm built and drew closer. Fizzles of lightning lit up the sky, miles away. The weather had been near-perfect since I'd arrived in Thistledew, and I could sense that the weather gods were preparing to unleash all the rain and stormy anger they had been storing up throughout spring. The sky owed us, and now it was ready to pay up.

Bear hadn't slept all day; I could tell he was on edge because of the weather. They say dogs are intuitive, and I think ours had enough sense to know that we should not be sitting out here in the middle of this mess. But, like the perfect dog he was, he remained faithfully beside me with his head in my lap, keeping me from dwelling on the fact that I was currently sitting—suspended on an ancient, partially rotted wooden and metal staircase—twenty feet off the ground in the middle of the biggest storm I'd ever witnessed in my life.

While I watched the green-and-black sky shift and morph and grow into something that was somehow both ugly and beautiful, I couldn't help but think of Amelia. My sister loved thunderstorms, but she was also terrified of them. Whenever thunder cracked, she'd dive under my legs and scream. Then, seconds later, she'd peek out and grin, her face lit up with the most enormous smile. "That was cool," she almost always declared, like thunder was a novelty. She'd sit, tense and terrified, through the whole of the storm, then run outside to search for a rainbow. That was Amelia— even things that scared her were thrilling. She always managed to maintain the belief that even the most awful experiences had the potential to end with something beautiful.

Throughout this summer, I had come to realize that my sister would figure out how to pull through this horrible tragedy in a way only Amelia could. Once she was out of the hospital, she would certainly understand the horror of what had happened to her and what still lay ahead, but I hoped she would also be able to see that life would move on.

And I was ready to help her figure it out. My time for grieving and being scared and drowning in my own guilt was over. Now my family needed me to be strong and come back ready to rebuild. Our life as we knew it—Amelia's especially—had been destroyed, but it wasn't gone. That's what I had to focus on, in order to help us all move forward.

I'd been absentmindedly rubbing Bear's back and

thinking about my beautiful sister when suddenly, I sensed the big dog's shoulder blades tensing. His ears pricked, and the hair on his neck stood up in a ridge. A low growl came from deep inside his chest. He stared out into the wilderness, looking alert.

"What's up, good boy?" I asked.

Suddenly, a bright streak of lightning shot out of the clouds and sizzled toward the ground. Seconds later, the sharp crack of thunder followed. As soon as it did, Bear shot up with a yelp. Terrified by the sound and the sensation, he ran down the tower stairs and shot off into the woods.

"Bear!" I screamed, running down the stairs faster than I ever had before. I raced to the edge of the woods where he'd disappeared. "Bear! Come!"

But he didn't come.

I called again, but I heard nothing in response. Another shot of lightning zigzagged out of the clouds, and another loud clap of thunder chased after it. Finally, I heard Bear bark, somewhere out in the woods, and I hollered again. "Bear! Here, buddy! Come, Big Bear!"

I didn't realize the rain had started until I felt Grandpa's warm hand on my shoulder and saw that his face was streaked with water. "Where'd he go?" Grandpa asked.

I pointed into the woods, at the spot where I'd watched Bear bound through the undergrowth and into the maze of trees.

"I'll go after him," Grandpa said.

"I'm coming with you," I said, heading after him toward

the woods. "Two of us will have a better chance of finding him."

Grandpa turned to face me, his hands solid on my shoulders. "You need to wait here," he said calmly. "If he follows our scent and comes back, he'll need to find you here or he's going to leave again. And, Maia? I need you to wait for us on the tower stairs. The storm is close, and if lightning strikes, I can't have you standing out here in the open. Those stairs and the tower itself are the only spots that are safe in this storm."

"I need to find Bear," I sobbed, only then realizing I'd begun to cry.

"You need to be here," Grandpa told me again. "I know you *want* to chase after him, but what Bear needs is for you to stay right here and be waiting to comfort him when he comes back." He took a deep breath. "And remember, your sister needs me to return you home to her in one piece. This is one of those times where you need to think about what others need from *you*, not what will make you feel better."

"Okay," I said. Then I shoved him toward the forest. "Please find him, Pops. You have to." I wanted to make him promise, but I knew no one could make that kind of promise. I just had to trust that he'd do everything he could to find him. And because it was Grandpa, I knew he would.

"I love that dog, Maia," he said, flashing me a small smile. "I'll get him home."

CHAPTER TWENTY-ONE

As soon as Grandpa disappeared into the cloak of trees, I raced back to the tower stairs and tentatively climbed up the first few steps. For once, I wanted to be up higher, where I could possibly get a glimpse of Bear dashing through the trees below. I closed my eyes and took another step. Then another. Finally, I reached the first stair landing and collapsed in a heap. Six more flights of stairs stretched above me, but this was as high off the ground as I could will myself to go without Grandpa or Bear by my side. I could see across the tops of the trees, but enough leaves had grown in that I quickly realized I wouldn't be able to see Bear racing along the ground, no matter *how* high I climbed. So I stayed put, convincing myself that it was best to wait for him where he could see me.

Thankfully, Grandpa had assured me that I was relatively safe from a lightning strike anywhere within the confines of the tower. I didn't like the idea of lightning hitting the tower and setting my hair on end or giving me any type of shock, but it beat the alternative—standing on top of the rock, serving as a human lightning rod.

All around the fire tower, the storm was raging. Luckily, despite my long list of fears, I'd never been afraid of thunderstorms. Maybe it was because Amelia *was*; I'd always had to be the strong sister during storms.

Strangely, even with a sky full of lightning and thunder, there was still only a light, gentle rain coming down. It made the storm feel even stronger and more powerful; like the clouds were holding back all that water, waiting to unleash it when they were good and ready.

Between cracks of thunder, I listened for the sound of Bear's barking. Once, I thought I heard his familiar yap coming from somewhere near the trail that led from the road up to the hill. I turned to look that way, then closed my eyes. I'd read somewhere that when you close down one of your senses, the others pick up the slack and become more finely tuned. With my eyes closed, I focused on listening again. This time, I was sure I heard his bark, but it seemed a bit farther off than I'd originally thought—if I had to guess, I'd say he was somewhere just east of the trail, about halfway between the fire tower and Grandpa's motorcycle. That was the direction Grandpa Howard had gone when he took off after him. I hoped Pops could hear the barking, too . . . good ol' Bear was helping our search efforts by giving us something to follow.

I watched the clouds shifting and rolling across the sky. They reminded me of my friend Anne's lava lamp, the way they morphed and grew and lit up with each lightning strike. Every few minutes, a streak of lightning shot out of a cloud and zigzagged through the inky sky; seconds later, another sharp crack of thunder would follow.

Waiting for Grandpa to return with Bear was torture. I felt helpless, just sitting under cover of the fire tower stairs, but I also felt vulnerable, perched way up here at the top of the world.

As I stared out at the spot where I'd last heard Bear's bark ring out, I suddenly noticed a snaking tendril of what looked like wispy fog curling up and out of the trees. For a split second, I just stared at it, mesmerized. Then every one of my senses jumped into action. Suddenly, I could see it, feel it, and for a second, I was almost certain I could smell it.

Smoke.

It seemed impossible. For weeks, Grandpa and I had been coming out here, waiting to spot any sign of a forest fire, but other than the one brush fire that had gotten a little bigger than it should have, we hadn't seen anything even close. Yet it was entirely possible today. Like Grandpa said, conditions were perfect for a fire; even Smokey Bear had warned us— for the past week, his sign on the side of the road had said FIRE DANGER: HIGH.

I stood up, for once not noticing that the solid ground was a full story below me. I scanned the tree line, hoping I'd been imagining it. But no, there it was, exactly where I'd first seen it. Just east of the trail, somewhere between the fire tower and town. It was curling out of a small valley, twisting up and out of the trees. I couldn't see any flames, but there was no mistaking the telltale sign of the first stage of a fire.

For a moment, my breath got stuck in my throat, and I felt myself choking. I was transported back to my house, watching as my sister fell victim to the flames. Too often, I could still smell the fire, like the smoke had never fully left my body. It was just lurking, smoldering, deep inside my lungs, waiting to come out and terrify me again and again and again.

I grabbed the wooden handrail and braced myself. I needed to call it in. Grandpa wasn't in the tower, and surely all the Beaver planes that kept watch for fires had been grounded because of the storm. No one else would have spotted it. No one else would spot it until the fire caught and flashed over and began to burn everything in its path.

Tentatively, I put a foot on the next step and began to climb. About halfway up the second set of stairs, I thought of the narrow path, my only way out of the forest. If the fire spread from where I'd seen the smoke, if the wind shifted, I could be trapped. Walled in by fire, watching as the forest blazed up around me, choking off my escape route. Surrounded by hungry flames as the trees lit up in a massive bonfire around the tower.

But I willed myself to keep climbing. Grandpa and Bear were out there somewhere, and I couldn't abandon them. They had no idea what was building around them, that a fire was coming for them. There was no warning.

Up and up and up I climbed, looking only forward. I focused on breathing, and not thinking of what was happening out in the forest, paying attention to nothing beyond the here and now. I was only halfway up, and the radio was all the way at the top. From the top, I knew, I'd be able to get a better view of where exactly the smoke was coming from. Then I could call it in. Grandpa had told me how the radio worked, but to use it, I had to climb every step.

My feet froze on the fourth set of stairs. My body tensed, and my breath stopped. I closed my eyes and thought of Bear. Of Grandpa. Of Amelia. All helpless, relying on me.

I looked out over the rail on the fifth-story landing and noticed that the fire had already grown. From down below, it had seemed no bigger than a mere tendril. But from up here, I could see that the smoke was much broader at its base. I knew how quickly fire could spread in these conditions, and with the wind whipping the way it was, a fire left to spread would be capable of destroying acres before anyone could contain it.

The faint sound of Bear's bark shook me out of my terrified stupor. He barked again; a warning. I got down on my hands and knees, vowing to *crawl* the rest of the way up to the tower if that's what I had to do. I could not, would not, leave Bear and Grandpa out there. With my eyes closed, I slithered up the rest of the stairs and collapsed through the door of the fire tower. I didn't look around, just crawled over the rough wooden floor on my hands and knees and grabbed for the radio hanging in the middle of the far wall.

As I dialed it in, waiting for someone from the Forest Service to pick up on the other side, I peered out the window and caught the first glimpse of flames stretching up out of a stand of pines. "Help!" I croaked into the radio. "We need help."

CHAPTER TWENTY-TWO

The old radio communicator crackled to life. "Howard?" a voice asked.

"This is his granddaughter Maia," I said breathlessly into the mouthpiece. "I saw smoke. My grandpa and our dog are out in the woods, and I saw smoke." There was a short pause, probably while someone tried to figure out why a kid was on the other end of their radio. But there wasn't time for pauses. I knew all too well that seconds and minutes could mean everything in a situation like this. "Hello?"

"Got it, Maia," said the voice. "Where did you see the smoke? Can you describe the location?"

Thanks to Grandpa's lesson in compass skills, I was pretty confident about which direction was which from each side of the old fire tower. "Just east of the trail that leads down to the highway from the fire lookout," I told the person on the other end of the line. "About halfway between the tower and the road."

Again, a pause. This time, I hoped, they were consulting a map. "How much smoke is there?"

I tried to remain calm. Panic wasn't going to help anyone out of this situation. For once, I didn't feel the need to puke and thanked my lucky stars for that. I was gonna need all those lucky stars today. "A few minutes ago, it was just a small trail of smoke. But now, from up here at the top of the tower, I can see there are some flames." Then, for good measure, I added, "It's dry out there."

"Got it," the voice replied. "We're sending a couple crews out right away. Maia, you're in the tower now?"

"Yes."

"And where's Howard?"

"Our dog got spooked by the storm," I said. "He bolted. Grandpa went after him." I thought about telling the person on the other end that Grandpa had *forced* me to stay behind; that I had *wanted* to help look for Bear, but he'd made me sit and wait.

But before I could, the voice said, "I'm glad you stayed back to keep watch. It's a good thing someone was up there to spot the smoke. With conditions like these, even with today's rain, this could catch and spread real quick."

"Yeah," I said. "I know."

"But now I need you to leave," said the voice. "Do you know the way out? Can you hike out on your own?"

"I know the way," I said. "But I can't leave without my grandpa. And Bear."

"Maia, listen to me. That fire is much too close to your location for you to stay put. With the direction the wind is blowing right now, it's safe for you to evacuate. But that might not be true in an hour or so."

I heard what this faceless person on the other end of the radio was telling me: If I didn't leave now, I might not get out.

"We'll have crews out there in less than ten minutes,

Maia. They're better equipped to look for Howard and get him to safety. I'm gonna call your grandma Bea and tell her to drive out and pick you up at the bottom of the trail. We need to get you out of the line of fire, or you're no use at all to your grandpa or your dog."

I looked out at the forest, at that beautiful sea of green and brown spreading out all around me. The horizon blended right into the storm-filled sky, which was still rolling in greens and purples and bruise-black clouds. Facing east, I could see the flames even more clearly now. They'd grown. I could easily imagine what it smelled and sounded like down on the ground, near the fire. The sharp whistle as the fire gobbled up the surrounding air; the crackle and snap as the flames sparked dry, dead undergrowth; the whoosh of a tree getting caught up in the arms of the blaze.

It wasn't nearly as close as it had been that night at home, but I wasn't foolish enough to think this fire was any less dangerous. If there were a sudden shift in the wind, it could be upon me. I had to decide—stay and search for Grandpa? Or get out . . .

I didn't have to think long to know what Grandpa would want me to do. Those crews needed me out of here. They couldn't focus on their job—controlling the fire—if I were out here, willingly putting myself in harm's way. I had to go. It's not what I wanted to do, but it's what I needed to do.

"Maia?" the voice said. "Are you still there?"

"Yes," I answered. "But I'm leaving now."

Then I clicked the radio back into place and fled down the

stairs. I didn't allow myself time for fear as I raced down those steep, rickety steps. Somehow, they didn't seem nearly as terrifying anymore. I'd made it up once; now I knew I could survive the climb.

At the base of the tower, I dashed across the bald rock face and dove into the forest. My legs burned as I jumped over roots and raced down the path I'd come to know so well. It was like my muscles were working on memory, guiding me down the trail and out toward the road.

But when I was about halfway down the path, halfway to where I'd meet Grandma Bea in her car, I heard a bark—Bear. I knew he was somewhere very close. I stopped to get my bearings, trying to figure out which way was which. Down here, buried inside the mess of forest and trees, it was hard to tell which direction was north.

But then I felt it—*fire*.

Just as I'd felt it that night, when Amelia and I had been home alone, I felt it now. Maybe some part of me could smell it, or maybe I heard it, but I'm pretty sure there was something about the air that just *felt* different somehow. Something was off; it didn't feel the same as it usually did when we were coming up this path.

Bear barked again. It wasn't his usual friendly greeting—this bark sounded more urgent. I could hear him clearly, just east of the trail. He wasn't far. The bark was near enough that I was pretty sure he was only a few hundred yards away from where I'd stopped my descent.

The fire crews would be here soon, and I was almost to

the road. But in a split-second decision that I knew I might later regret, I left the trail and pushed into the woods. Spindly tree limbs cut gashes into my arms and whipped at my face, and downed branches scratched at my ankles and legs. But I didn't notice any of it . . . all I focused on was the sound of Bear's barking. His call came every ten seconds or so, just a short yap, a repeated cry for help.

I plunged through the trees, calling to him. "Bear! Come!" The lightning and thunder had finally stopped, but rain was coming down in a steady drizzle now. Though the sky was still dark from the storm, I could see clearly enough to pick a trail through the woods. "Here, boy!"

Bear's cries grew closer and closer, until finally I came upon him. He was soaking wet and there were burrs stuck all over his legs, and tangled up in his soft, mangy belly fur. But he didn't seem injured, and he even offered me one of his giant-tail-wag hellos and a little doggy smile. "Bear!" I cried, falling to my knees to pull him close. "We gotta get you out of here, pal. Where's Grandpa?"

He pulled away from me, then barked again. I'd started to turn to head back toward the main trail, but Bear just stood stock still, looking at me. Then he turned and ran farther east, deeper into the forest. Even as a hint of smoke tickled at my nose, coming from the direction Bear had run, I chased after him. Through a tightly packed grove of white pine, over a collection of fallen birch trees, heading so deep into the forest that I worried I might never find my way out again.

That's when we came upon Grandpa Howard. He was sitting on the ground, bleeding, with his pant leg torn from knee to ankle. And cursing up a storm.

"Pops! What happened?" I asked.

Grandpa looked up, obviously startled to see me. "Trying to keep up with that damn dog, I stepped funny and twisted my ankle real good. Then I sliced my leg open on a rock, and if I'm gonna say it in polite terms, it doesn't feel fantastic."

His leg looked awful—his pant leg was all bloody, and judging by the fact that the twisted ankle had taken Grandpa to the ground, I had a feeling he might have broken it. He wasn't the kind of guy who went down easily. "So much complaining for such a minor injury," I teased, holding my hand out to help him up. "Do you want me to cut the leg off? Then you won't feel the cut anymore."

"Cute," he grumbled, letting me pull him to his feet. Bear's ears had pricked up, and he barked at us to get a move on. Just as he'd sensed the storm, I suspected Bear could sense the fire that was now coming for us.

"So, here's the deal," I told Grandpa, wrapping his arm around my shoulder so he could lean against me and take the weight off his bad leg. "There's a forest fire that blazed up just east of here. We're about a quarter mile from the trail, then it's another half mile or so down to the road. Do you think you can make it that far, if I help you?"

"Do I have a choice?" he asked, wincing as he tested his bad leg.

"No." I took a deep breath in, and now I was almost

certain I could smell smoke. The fire was getting closer. I couldn't possibly predict exactly how much time we had before it was upon us, but I knew it wouldn't be long. "I called the smoke in, and the fire crew should be out here soon, if they're not already. But I don't really want to sit here and wait, hoping for a rescue."

"You called it in?" Grandpa asked, taking a few tentative steps to test how quickly he could walk now that he had me to lean on. Bear led the way, sniffing out our best path back through the brush.

"Yup," I said. His breathing was ragged and uneven beside me, so I decided I'd better try to keep his mind off the pain. "I didn't exactly have time to get a good look around, but you really *do* have a lot of cans of Spam up there in the tower."

Grandpa glanced at me, and I could tell from his expression that he was proud of me for climbing up—finally. But he wasn't the kind of guy to get sentimental and mushy on me, so instead he said, "Didn't happen to bring a can of that Spam with you, by any chance?" His voice was gruff as he struggled to walk through the pain. "I'm starving."

"Shoot," I said. "I guess I forgot the most important thing. You know, I *would* go back for it, but I've got this old man leaning on me, making bad jokes."

"Old man?" he muttered. "I'm *injured*. Not old." We walked in silence for a while, each of us struggling to hold the other up. Just as the trail came into view up ahead of us, Grandpa said, "Hey, kid? Thanks. I don't know how you found me, but I do know I wasn't going anywhere fast until you showed up."

"Bear found you," I told him. "Good thing you kept him around this summer, huh? Maybe he deserves a bed in the house now?"

"Well, we'll see about that." Grandpa leaned on me a little more as we started down the main trail. "But I'll tell you what—if we get out of here, I'll treat you both to a nice big dish of ice cream to say thanks for saving me. Ice cream's healthier than Spam, anyway."

"You've got a deal," I told him.

"Then lead the way, kid."

STAGES OF A FIRE

STAGE 4: DECAY (SMOLDERING, GLOWING)

With a decrease in fuel or oxygen, a fire smolders down to embers and ash. This is a dangerous phase, because an introduction of new fuel or an increase in oxygen could reinvigorate the fire. This is also usually the longest stage of a fire; it often takes weeks to fully extinguish all embers and begin the process of decay and regrowth.

CHAPTER TWENTY-THREE

The fire raged that afternoon. Crews were brought in from hundreds of miles away, quickly doubling, tripling, and quadrupling the population of Thistledew. The rain began in earnest around dinnertime, helping to keep the flames from spreading as quickly as they would have in dry weather. But after months of little to no rain, the forest was a welcome host to fire, and it continued to spread and smolder long into the night.

The crews fighting the blaze dug trenches and cut a fire line around the area, hoping to contain it. The Forest Service made the decision that this part of the forest was due for a fire, and since conditions were favorable—high humidity, decreasing winds, and cool, wet weather—they decided to allow for a controlled burn. The containment lines were drawn far outside town, and crews kept the fire from spreading up the hill near the fire tower. So me and Grandpa's part of the forest would be preserved, but much of the area around it would burn, making way for decay and new growth.

Grandpa Howard desperately wanted to help fight the fire, but they told him he was too injured to go out and help clear brush or actually battle the blaze (his ankle was sprained and he'd needed a few stitches where he'd sliced his leg open in the woods, but luckily he hadn't broken any bones). After Grandpa argued with and grumped at his old Forest Service pals—and even went so far as trying to sneak out on a truck with one of the fire crews—someone asked if Pops would be willing to help out at the fire communications command post. He reluctantly agreed to stay put in the Forest Service regional offices, where he could help direct crews and keep people informed about what was going on.

As always, I called my parents that night to check on my sister and tell them about the day's events. Amelia was doing much better—her fever had broken, the infection was gone, and she was actually awake and alert enough to be on the FaceTime call with my parents while I told my story. For the first time since I'd left home, I saw her face. The burns had left her scarred and somewhat unfamiliar-looking, and under the thin bandage-hat on her head, I knew that her hair was gone altogether. She was wearing a soft T-shirt, not a hospital gown, which gave me hope that she was moving back toward a more normal life. That maybe she'd eventually get to leave the hospital. It was a relief to see some of the old spark still in her eyes, and I was filled with total joy when I heard her laugh as I told them about the Spam collection up in Grandpa's fire tower.

"I'm so glad you're safe," Mom said after I'd finished the whole story, her voice thick with emotion. I noticed then that my sister had drifted off, asleep and peaceful in her crisp white bed. She would be moving from the hospital's burn unit to a rehab facility very soon, where specialized staff would continue to help with her recovery from the burns, and she'd have even more frequent physical therapy to help get her body moving again. She still had a cast on her leg, but once that came off, the PT would also help get her legs back in shape after the break and so much time in bed. "We have something to tell you, too," Mom said quietly, so as not to wake Amelia. "The fire department's arson investigator finally confirmed the official cause of the fire today."

I held my breath, waiting. This was the conversation I'd been avoiding for weeks. "They're one hundred percent confident the fire was caused by faulty wiring in the basement," Dad said. "That's what they'd been assuming, but because the damage to the back half of the house was so severe, it took some time for them to confirm it for certain."

"It wasn't my candle?" I asked, my voice barely a whisper.

"It definitely wasn't your candle," Mom said. She and Dad shared a look, then she turned back to me. "Maia, honey, Grandma told us about your conversation yesterday. I had no idea you've been holding on to this kind of guilt about what happened."

I didn't say anything. I didn't think I *could*.

Dad said, "Just so you know, I've blamed myself plenty of times, too, kiddo."

"Why?" I choked out.

"I'm the one who wanted a new electrical panel," he said. "If it weren't for me, they wouldn't have been playing with the wiring in the walls. Houses like ours, with old electrical systems, are usually fine—until someone starts fiddling with them and knocking things loose."

"And I can't stop wondering what might have happened that night if I hadn't left you girls alone," Mom added. "I'm also the only one who knew the contractors had disconnected some of our wiring that week while they worked. I should have checked the smoke detector battery. That's all on me." Her voice got husky, and even though the connection on the video wasn't great, I could tell she'd begun to cry. "There are so many what-ifs, Maia. So many."

"It's not all on you," Dad said, pulling Mom close.

I nodded. The three of us all sat there quietly for a few moments. "None of us is to blame," I said finally. "It was a fluke. A terrible accident." I thought about what Grandpa and I had talked about that morning on the way up to the fire tower. I couldn't believe we'd had that conversation less than twenty-four hours ago! "The only thing we can do now is stop wondering what might have happened if things had gone differently, and figure out how to move on from here."

Mom glanced at Dad, then they both nodded. "You're absolutely right, Maia," Mom said, sniffling. "It doesn't help anyone if we keep dwelling on it."

Dad sighed. "But it's definitely hard not to keep going over and over everything and wish I could go back and change so many things leading up to that night," he said softly. It felt reassuring, somehow, to hear my parents—two smart adults—sounding uncertain and scared and guilty. I wasn't alone.

"Maia makes a good point," Mom said, as much to me as to Dad. "We all have things we wish we could change about what happened. But it's pointless and harmful to look back, since we can't rewind time. All we can do now is focus on what's ahead of us. We all have a lot of healing to do, and we should be focusing our energy and time on that."

We sat on the call for a while longer, saying nothing more, just thinking and being together as a family. Before we hung up, Dad told me he was going to book a ticket to fly in the next afternoon. I was excited to see him without a screen between us and talk to him about all of this more in person, and just give him a hug. I also couldn't wait to introduce him to Bear and Wilma and Griffin.

The next morning, when Grandma went to pick Dad up at the Hibbing airport, I stayed behind to cuddle with Bear— who was still totally exhausted from his big adventure in the forest and the brushing and bath he'd been subjected to afterward—and keep watch over Wilma. I also stayed back because it was my and Griffin's last day of swimming lessons, and I didn't want to miss it. Wendy drove us out to the lake a little early, so the three of us could have a picnic dinner on the sand and watch as the swim instructors and a lifeguard set up the inflatable climbing wall and slide out past the buoys.

From the moment we arrived at the lake, Griffin was bursting with excitement. He'd finally gotten comfortable paddling almost to the edge of the swim area *without* his life jacket on, and he could tread water longer than anyone else taking summer lessons. Because I'd vowed to support him through this journey, I could do all this now, too. So both Griffin and I had earned ourselves a ticket out to the climbing wall and slide as a prize for passing our swim tests.

The twins, on the other hand, had not. Ellen and Hannah still refused to even *try* to get in the water without life jackets, despite the fact that their mom kept yelling at them from shore to "just *try*!" They told Griffin and me they planned to skip the last class, rather than watch the rest of us get to celebrate and play out in the water on the inflatable slide. Griffin and I felt proud, being the only two from our swim group who had actually passed the course.

When it was time for our final session to start, Evan headed over to collect me and Griffin from the beach. "You ready?" he asked, high-fiving each of us. "Griff, bud, you feeling good about swimming out to collect your prize?"

Griffin glanced at me, and I gave him an encouraging nod. "I can't wait," he said. "But if I decide I don't want to slide down or jump off the top of the climbing wall, is that okay?"

"You do whatever you're comfortable with, pal," Evan said, grinning. "I—and Jenna and Anika, the two lifeguards—will be out there the whole time, to make sure you're safe. I just want you to get to celebrate how much you've learned this summer. Remember how you were afraid to even *float* in the lake when we first started this class?"

"I remember." Griffin laughed.

Next, Evan looked to me. "And, Maia, are you feeling ready?" He wiggled his eyebrows, and his big shaggy beard wiggled along. "Have you thought about what I suggested, about maybe trying to swim a little farther, all the way out to the wooden raft?"

"Let's see how *this* swim goes first, okay?" I answered.

Evan laughed. "Fair enough."

Slowly, Griffin and I waded into the water. Griffin yelped when the chilly water splashed up to his belly button, and again when he was up to his armpits. But we both kept going, side by side, and eventually, we were happily treading water out in the part of the swimming area where we could no longer touch. "Ready?" I asked Griffin.

"Let's do this," he said. Then he took a deep breath and put his face in the water. Awkwardly, he started paddling a messy front crawl out toward the giant inflatable slide. I swam along beside him, holding my own head above water so I could keep an eye on him. I knew Evan and Anika and Jenna were nearby, too—each pulling a floating ring on a rope, just in case either of us got tired and needed a break—but it made me feel better to have my eyes on Griffin, too.

At the edge of the marked swimming area, we paused. Griffin and I each grabbed the slimy rope strung up between the line of buoys. All that was left was to duck under the rope and we'd be there. I lifted the rope high above the surface of the lake, so Griffin could swim underneath first. Two easy strokes later, he grabbed the edge of the big, inflatable slide and pulled himself up and out of the lake. "Yes!" he hollered, pumping his fists. "We made it!"

I scrambled up beside him, and Griff wrapped his arms around me in a wet hug. Then we both started to climb up to the top of the big inflatable climbing wall. At first, we kept sliding off, falling back into the water or onto the bouncy surface down below. But after a few tries, Griffin managed to get to the top, and I wasn't far behind. The best part was sliding down the inflatable slide attached to the climbing wall, landing with a plop in the huge lake below.

After lots of turns, Griffin decided he needed a little rest and lay down in the sun at the tippy-top part of the wall. Evan looked at me. "What do you think? You want to keep going to the wooden raft?" He winked. "I wouldn't let you try if I thought you couldn't swim that far. But I need to make sure *you* think you're ready to do it . . ."

I nodded. "I'm as ready as I'll ever be." This wasn't entirely true; I wasn't an exceptional swimmer. There was plenty of room for me to improve my skills and confidence in the water. But I was good *enough* that I knew I could probably swim to the raft without any real struggle. And the more important thing was that I felt ready. A few weeks ago, there was no way I would have attempted a swim challenge like this. But now, after everything else I'd dealt with this spring and summer, swimming out to the raft actually felt achievable.

"Will you be okay here by yourself?" I called up to Griffin.

"I've got Anika to keep me company," Griffin replied, giving the lifeguard a thumbs-up. As I set off, heading out into an even deeper part of the lake, Griffin cheered me on. This really helped keep me going whenever I felt tempted to turn around and give up. But after all those hikes up to the tower, and our swim lessons with Evan, I was in pretty great physical shape and soon found my natural rhythm in the water. I took long, slow, steady strokes, just the way Evan had taught me, and was careful to breathe to the side—rather than lifting my whole torso up and out of the water with each breath—to help conserve my energy. (This strategy also kept my legs from dropping down into the murky depths below, where I still worried there were enormous fish waiting to munch on my toes.)

When I flipped onto my back to get my bearings and take a few easy breaths—just like I'd done with Grandma when we were in our floating diapers—I saw that I was already more than halfway to my goal. A few of the older swimmers were waiting for me out on the raft, and everyone was cheering. With a smile, I rolled back over onto my stomach and continued my victory swim.

As I pulled through the final stretch, I considered how much both my sister and I had gone through this summer. Until now, Amelia's healing had been mostly physical. Mine was a summer of emotional healing that had ended with huge physical challenges. The cool thing was, as I swam out into the middle of the lake all by myself, I could actually see and feel how much I'd changed.

I'd decided to ask my parents about starting counseling when I got home, to help me work through some of my other worries and fears. A few of my friends saw therapists, and I'd realized that without having the space and calm of the fire tower and forest back home, I had to figure out different ways of dealing with stuff. I knew that one summer couldn't totally change who I was, deep down, but being in Thistledew—away from my regular life and forced to act like Maia the Brave—had certainly helped me start to realize the person I was capable of becoming.

Suddenly, my hand hit the edge of the raft. Above me, some of the older swimmers were clapping and whooping and pointing to the ladder so I could climb up and join them. With a huge, exhausted breath, I rolled onto the wooden raft and lifted my arms in the air like a hero. I looked back at Griffin, who was waving to me from his perch on top of the inflatable climbing wall. Then I glanced toward shore, where Wendy was pumping her arms in the air and hollering out congratulations. That's when I saw two familiar people jogging across the beach from the parking lot. My dad and Grandma had made it in time to witness my big victory! They both waved to me, and I waved back, giving them a big thumbs-up.

I stood in the center of the old wooden raft for a moment,

taking in my surroundings and congratulating myself. Smoke that had drifted for miles from the forest fire cast everything in a sort of foggy, magical haze. Warm late-afternoon sun beat down on the tips of the cedar and white pine trees lining the edge of the lake, bathing them in an orange glow. The water glittered around me.

As I curled my toes around the edge of the wooden platform, preparing to jump back into the water and return to Griffin, I realized something: I was ready to go home. I'd miss Grandpa Howard and Grandma Bea, Griffin and Bear, and of course little Wilma. But it was time. I needed to go. And now, I knew, I was really and truly *ready*. Ready to support my family, whenever *they* were ready to begin the emotional healing that would come next. If my parents didn't have room in their hotel room for me, I'd already talked to Beckett and Anne, and they'd both said their families were happy to have me take turns staying with each of them so I could be closer to my sister.

It was time.

With a big smile, I took a deep breath, closed my eyes, and jumped—cannonballing into deep water. For the first time in forever, I wasn't scared of the unknown.

CHAPTER TWENTY-FOUR

Three Months Later

"How do you know which one she is?" Amelia stood on top of my feet, trying to make herself taller, so she had a better view over the fence at the deer sanctuary.

"I don't know," I admitted. We'd stopped to visit Wilma on our way from the airport to Grandma and Grandpa's house. Amelia and I both had a long weekend off school for fall break, and Mom and Dad had been the ones to suggest we use the time to visit our Thistledew family. I couldn't wait to get back. I'd been missing Big Bear and Griffin and Grandma and Grandpa like crazy.

Amelia had asked me to tell and retell the stories from my summer in Minnesota so many times that I knew the memories would be imprinted on my mind forever. But I felt like Amelia couldn't truly appreciate the stories until she'd spent time with my summer family herself. I also knew that a little time in the fresh Minnesota air, away from her doctors and physical therapists and checkups, would do her good.

Together, my sister and I peered over the fence and looked at a trio of smallish deer who were grazing on some grass not very far away. Honestly, they all looked pretty much the same to me: fluffy white tails, soft brown fur, skinny legs. Even their eyes were all the same color. I don't know why I thought I would be able to recognize Wilma as soon as I saw her, but it was now pretty obvious I wouldn't. In the months since I'd last seen her, she'd grown from fawn to a nearly-full-sized deer, and unlike then, she was now entirely capable of feeding herself. "I honestly don't know what she would look like now that she's not scrawny and small anymore."

"How many deer live at the sanctuary?" Amelia asked me, clutching my hand.

I was still getting used to the feel of her new skin, which would always be severely scarred after the fire. Some parts of her body still looked pretty much the way they did before that May night, but one of her hands and arms had been burned very badly, as had a lot of her skin that was usually hidden by clothes. The skin grafting surgeries had helped to cover up some of her worst burns, but even those areas would never look like they did before the fire. Also, her hair was still growing back rough and patchy after it, too, had caught in the blaze. Luckily, Amelia had always been a confident kid and didn't seem too worried about what she looked like. And even *more* luckily, the fire hadn't destroyed her spirit. At her core, she was still the same incredible girl she'd always been.

"I think there are a couple dozen deer living here most of the time," I replied. "Most of them are rescues, like Wilma, but Griffin told me a few were born here at the sanctuary." Griffin had been volunteering at the deer sanctuary every Saturday morning, so he could keep a close eye on Wilma and continue his research on deer and other wildlife. He'd definitely found the perfect place to utilize his special blend of patience, kindness, intelligence, and love for animals.

My parents were standing behind me and my sister, hovering, the way they often did with Amelia these days. She had spent most of the summer in the rehab center and tucked away inside the small, rented house we would be living in until our own house was ready for us again, but when school started up in the fall, she'd insisted she was ready to go. I knew she was, but my parents had been more wary about sending her anywhere.

"Does Wilma have any distinctive marks?" Mom asked. She hadn't ever met her, but Dad had—during the two days he and I had spent together in Thistledew, before we left to return home together.

"She had a ton of little white spots," I said. "But those disappear as a fawn gets older. Most deer lose their spots entirely before they're a year old."

A few large deer stood and stared at us from a distance, looking almost eerie because of the way they lurked, stone-still, statues hidden among the trees of the sanctuary. No humans were allowed beyond the fence line, since it would make the area less hospitable to the deer who were kept here for their own safety.

"Now I can understand where the phrase 'like a deer caught in headlights' comes from," Dad murmured. "It's like they're frozen."

"They're pretty," Amelia said. "I wish I could touch one."

"I wish you could, too," I said, remembering the downy softness of Wilma's newborn hide, tucked and curled inside her hay bed. "You would have loved feeding Wilma from her bottle."

"Tell me the story again, about when Grandma and Grandpa let you sleep next to her in the shed?" Amelia begged.

"Later," I promised. "We can make a fort inside the shed, where her bed was hidden, and I'll tell you the story in there. That will help you picture the scene more clearly."

"Okay," Amelia said. "And you promise I can hang out with Griffin, too, right? And Bear is still there?"

"As far as I know," I told her. According to Griffin, as soon as I left, Grandpa let Bear start sleeping inside the house. He said Bear pretty much only leaves the house to go up to the fire tower with Grandpa Howard during the day, and when Grandma lets him out for his last-chance pee at night. Otherwise he just snoozes in Grandpa's old recliner in the corner of the den. *My room*, I thought. *Big Bear sleeps in my room.*

"Let's go," Amelia said suddenly. "I want to get there so I can meet him. I hope he sleeps in bed with us tonight."

I looked out into the vast deer sanctuary again, whispering a silent *"hello and I love you and miss you"* to Wilma, wherever she was. Then I blew a kiss at those frozen deer and reminded myself that she was better off with a pack of deer than she would have been if we'd kept her in the backyard of the Thistledew house forever.

Just as I was turning to go to make the short trek back to our rental car so we could move on to Grandma and Grandpa's house, another small pack of deer emerged from a thick grove of trees. There was the tiniest gap in the branches, and a faint curving trail on the ground where the deer had carved a natural path through the forest. These four joined the others to stare at us, but then one of the smallest deer stepped forward. It continued to walk toward us, stopping every couple of steps, then carrying on.

When it was a few feet away, just on the other side of the fence, it froze. As soon as I looked into its eyes, I knew. "Wilma," I breathed.

My sister took my hand again. "Is that her?" she asked, staring at the little deer in front of us.

I nodded. Wilma took another step forward, and I moved up to meet her at the fence. She lowered her head and touched her nose to the ground, right near my feet, on the other side of the fence. I wanted nothing more than to reach out and stroke her back, touch her soft hide, but I resisted. She wasn't mine, and Griffin had taught me that human scent could warn off the other deer, and maybe even make them reject her from the herd. Instead, I reached down and touched the ground, on my own side of the fence.

We locked eyes. Wilma blinked, and I smiled. Then she turned and walked back to her pack, leaving me with mine. It was hard to say goodbye, since I didn't know if I'd ever see her again. But because we'd been there for each other during some of the hardest moments in each of our lives, I knew that no matter what, Wilma and I would always be family.

• • •

We pulled up to Grandma and Grandpa's house just before dinner. Griffin was sitting on the lawn with Bear, waiting for us; I had a feeling he'd been there for quite a while. Amelia bounded out of the car and raced over, squealing with delight as she got down on the ground and rubbed Big Bear's ears and back. He greeted her just as enthusiastically, wagging and smiling and sniffing at her face, which gave me opportunity to give Griffin a big hug.

"Guess what?" he said, squirming out of my arms almost immediately. "The Cub Scout badge ceremony is tonight! And Mom said, since you're here this weekend, you can come!" I loved that Griffin was the kind of person who could jump right back into an easy friendship, as if no time had passed at all since we'd last been together. He looked to my parents, then Amelia. I was relieved that he didn't stare at my sister's scars. Some people—many people—*did* stare, and it always made me uncomfortable. Luckily, Amelia seemed unfazed by people's questioning looks, and often she even told people what had happened. The kid amazed me.

Griffin went on, "I mean, you're *invited*, but you only have to come if you want. Amelia could come, too. There's a potluck dinner, and our den leader always brings walking tacos, which are the best food ever. You get to open a bag of

225

chips and just pour all the other taco stuff—like meat and cheese and lettuce and sour cream and stuff—right inside the chip bag, then you walk around while you eat it with a fork. Mom and I made brownies to bring, and there's usually a ton of other desserts."

I glanced at my sister, who was already nodding enthusiastically. "I think it sounds fun," she declared. "And I love walking tacos."

Just then, Grandma hustled out the front door and ran over to greet us all. She gave Amelia a long, gentle hug, obviously aware that squeezing too hard would hurt her. "I'm so excited to have you all here for the weekend," she said. She waggled her skinny eyebrows at my mom. "I made my famous stew, since I know it's your favorite."

Mom and I exchanged a look. We'd talked about Grandma's mystery-meat stew plenty of times since I'd come home from my summer in Thistledew, and I knew it was very much *not* Mom's favorite. It was no one's favorite. I had survived the summer by picking vegetables out of the nest of stringy meat, then sopping up as much of the gravy as I could stomach with several of Grandma's delicious buttered rolls. But Mom had to pretend she loved the stuff, since it was the polite thing to do—and Grandma had made it as a special treat, just for her. "Yum," Mom said with a weak smile. "I can't wait."

"Oh, shoot," I said, faking disappointment as I glanced from Grandma to Griffin. "Griffin just invited me and Amelia to his Cub Scout badge ceremony tonight. I don't want to ditch you guys on stew night, but . . ." Truth be told, I wasn't exactly sure what a Cub Scout ceremony entailed, but if it had anything to do with all the badges we'd worked on together this summer, I was totally in. Especially if it meant no stew. I asked Griffin, "Is this the night you get honored for all the badges you earned?"

"Yep," Griffin said.

"Go, go," Grandma said, with a wave of her hands. "You should both go. Wendy will be happy to have someone to keep her company during the dinner. And there's enough stew that we'll have leftovers for you to eat all weekend."

"Great," I muttered. I could tell Mom was trying to hold back her laughter "I can't wait. Save me a nice, meaty bowl full."

"Where's Dad?" Mom asked Grandma.

Just as she said it, I heard Grandpa's motorcycle growling down the road. "He was out at the fire tower," Grandma explained. "Can't seem to break the habit, especially after Maia spotted that smoke this summer. He'll be out there every day until it snows. To tell you the truth, he'd drive me a little nuts if he were just puttering around the house and yard all day, so I'm glad he has something to keep him busy."

Grandpa Howard pulled into the driveway, turned off his cycle, and unclasped his helmet. I hadn't seen or talked to him since I'd left Thistledew a few months earlier ("Your pops isn't much of a phone guy," Grandma had explained), and it felt great to see his scratchy flannel shirt and bright, smiling eyes again. He nodded at both Mom and Dad, said

"Hello, kiddo," to Amelia and ruffled her patchy hair, then strode over and put his hand on my shoulder. "It's great to see you, kid." He took a deep breath and said, "I've missed you."

It was such a simple and small thing to say, but coming from Grandpa, the sentiment meant a lot. "I missed you, too, Pops."

Grandpa turned back to Amelia. "Want a ride on my cycle?" he asked.

Amelia grinned. "Yeah, I do!"

Mom and Dad began to protest, but Grandpa shook his head. "I'll be careful," he promised.

"Let her go," I urged my parents. "She'll be fine. She's gonna love it." I thought back to just a few months before, when I was terrified to get on the back of Grandpa's motorcycle. Not anymore. After this summer, I'd finally stopped letting my fears get the best of me. In fact, I hadn't thrown up from nerves since the night our house burned.

"Please?" Amelia begged.

Mom and Dad exchanged a look, then they both glanced to me for the official go-ahead. They'd been doing that a lot since I came home. They perform their duties as overprotective parents, while I fill the role of loving sister and best friend, helping to gauge what Amelia actually is and isn't ready for. Sometimes my opinions about things are overruled, but most of the time my parents trust me to help them make decisions about her healing process.

I'd returned from Grandma and Grandpa's house a much

stronger and more confident person than the girl who'd left, and my parents seemed to notice the change. I knew they were both relieved that they could finally hand off some of the day-to-day emotional support my sister needed to me. I kept Amelia company in the rehab center and tried to make her laugh through months of physical therapy. Because I was able to help with a lot of those things, Mom and Dad could spend part of their time focusing on their own healing and the rebuild of our house.

With a sigh, Mom nodded. "Have fun," she told my sister, helping to buckle her helmet.

"Remember to hold on tight," my dad said.

Squealing, Amelia took my place on the back of Grandpa Howard's motorcycle, laughing her loud, beautiful laugh as they set off toward town.

• • •

Later that night, my sister and I squeezed in at the end of a long banquet table, along with Wendy, Griffin, and a pack of squirming Cub Scouts of varying ages. We'd all finished eating our fill of walking tacos—empty chip bags and salsa and pieces of shredded cheese and lettuce were scattered all over the table and floors—and one of the den leaders had finally announced that it was time for the badge ceremony.

Griffin and the other scouts clapped and cheered as each kid went up to shake hands with den leaders for earning three or four new badges during the summer and early fall. After ten long minutes, just when I was starting to worry that they'd forgotten about Griffin and his huge achievement, one of the scout leaders held up his hand for quiet. "This year, one ambitious member of our den went above and beyond what was expected. I'm proud to welcome our friend Griffin to come up and accept a certificate for working on the requirements for *every single one* of the Bear Scout badges."

Wendy whooped and whistled as her son walked to the front of the room to shake his den leader's hand. Several of his den mates pounded on the table and hollered out congratulations, and Griffin beamed from ear to ear. After taking a gallant bow, he raced back to our end of the table.

His mom jumped out of her chair and pulled him in for a giant hug. "My brilliant boy," she said into the top of his head. I could see that she had tears in her eyes. "My smart, talented, amazing Griff." Wendy pulled back and smiled at him. I was grateful I could be there to witness Griffin's big moment. I knew how badly he'd wanted to make his mom proud, and there was no doubt he'd accomplished that. "I'm so proud of you for setting such a big goal, and then sticking to it. How lucky am I that I have such a motivated young man in my life?" Griffin beamed at his mom, and the love between them was so evident.

Under the table, Amelia reached for my hand. Then she turned and smiled at me, and I considered how lucky *I* was to be a part of so many amazing people's worlds. Even though the fire had destroyed a huge part of our old lives, it had also opened up space for new growth. Now Griffin, Big Bear, Wendy, and Wilma were a part of my family, and

Mom, Dad, Amelia, and I had all been gifted the chance to build a stronger relationship with Grandpa Howard and Grandma Bea.

Of course, I still couldn't help but wonder sometimes how our lives would have turned out if the fire had never started, or if I'd gotten my sister out sooner that night. But wonder was all I could do; this was the reality of our lives now, and I was grateful that we were all figuring out how to emerge from the ashes together.

CHAPTER TWENTY-FIVE

The next morning, while my parents relaxed with their coffee, Grandpa offered to take me and Amelia out to the fire tower for a late-fall hike, and to help him close up the lookout for the season. He suggested that he drive us both out to the trail in Grandma's Buick. But that didn't feel right, somehow.

"I have a different idea . . ." I began. "You could take me and Bear out on the back of the motorcycle first, drop us off at the trail, and then come back for Amelia. Bear and I can hike the trail to the tower by ourselves, and we'll meet up with you there."

"No," Mom called out from the living room, where she had obviously been eavesdropping on our conversation while pretending to read.

"Why not?" I asked. "Bear and I spent plenty of time in the woods alone this summer," I pointed out. "We even rescued Grandpa from a forest fire, remember?"

"She's right," Grandpa said. "Maia will be fine out in the woods for fifteen minutes while I come back into town to get her sister. Let the kid have her independence. She's a smart one, and she's totally capable out there in the woods."

I could hear my parents conferring quietly together in the other room.

Grandpa winked at me, then added loudly, "I'll give her a compass, just in case she gets lost."

"Maia doesn't know how to use a compass," Dad laughed.

Grandpa called out to my parents, "You have no idea how much she knows." He and I shared a smile.

"Okay," Mom said finally. "If Maia is okay with it, we are, too."

Grandma packed us a picnic, even though we'd just had breakfast. "You might get hungry," she said.

I muttered to Grandpa, "That's what all that Spam is for, right?"

"She shows her love with food," Grandpa told me with a shrug. "That's why I've got three years' worth of emergency canned food hidden up in the tower. She's never let a day go by where I head out there without a whole day's worth of meals to keep me from starving to death."

It felt like coming home, to get on the back on Grandpa's motorcycle again. With Bear in his little sidecar next to me, we rode out to the tower path, blasting the music of Boxcar Willie. I sang along to the familiar songs, wondering what Amelia would think of Grandpa's music. Knowing my sister, she'd probably want to download a bunch of country songs onto my phone after this trip.

When we got out to the trail, Bear and I hopped out. With a quick wave, Grandpa turned his cycle around and zoomed away again, leaving me and Bear alone in our woods. I reached down and rubbed the soft fur between his shoulder blades, then together, we set off up the trail.

As I hiked, I let my mind wander to the last time Big Bear and I had been out here together: leading and supporting an injured Grandpa Howard out of the woods, before the fire could catch us. Looking back, with the information only hindsight can bring, we'd never really been in a huge amount of danger that day; the fire had never burned as far as the trail. But if the winds had shifted, our story could easily have ended differently.

The thing I'd learned from Grandpa that summer, though, is that you can't control the things that are out of your power. You only have the power to control how you react to them. I was trying hard to stop dwelling on the what-ifs in every scary situation, and instead, to challenge myself to face my fears using some of the techniques I'd been working on in therapy since I'd gone home to Chicago.

"Hey, buddy," I said breathlessly to Big Bear as we hiked up the hill. "I've really missed you, you know?" I was trying to stay calm and cool as we hiked up to the tower together, even though this walk wasn't an easy one. It brought back a whole flood of memories and feelings. But one of the strategies my new therapist had recommended was to acknowledge my fears and emotions; let them flare up and be noticed, instead of trying to tamp them down and pretend they didn't exist. Sometimes, she'd told me, you had to face a fear and let it take hold in order to fight it.

I stopped for a quick rest, realizing I'd gotten a little out of shape now that I wasn't hiking up this trail every day anymore. Bear stopped and looked at me, waiting, his tongue hanging out of his mouth. As I sat on the fallen log I was using as a bench, I thought about some of the stuff

I'd slowly been coming to terms with: Maybe I could have been quicker to pull my sister from the blaze, but I also could have frozen up entirely; could have waited too long and been locked out of her room by a wall of fire; could have run from the house to save myself and left my sister to die. Considering the alternatives, I'm glad things ended the way they did. I made the best possible choice in a bad situation, and no amount of second-guessing was going to alter the outcome.

I hopped to my feet and we started up the trail again. Soon, the fire tower came into view. It loomed over me, equal parts frightening and familiar. I'd only been inside the little hut perched at the very top of the stairs once, the day of the fire. Since then, I'd wondered many times what would happen the next time I visited Thistledew.

Suddenly, I knew exactly what needed to happen.

Without giving myself time to chicken out, I headed straight for the bottom of the stairs and placed my foot on that first step. Then I began to climb. One foot in front of the other, until I'd reached the first stair landing. Bear followed but stayed a step or two behind, as if he were preparing to catch me if I fell.

I wouldn't fall.

I climbed the second set of steps, then the third, stopping to breathe whenever I felt my chest tighten.

The farther I climbed, the freer I felt. The crisp, cool autumn wind whipped around me when I took a break on the final stair landing, and the door that led into the little shelter at the top came into my sights up ahead of me. I didn't take time to look around at the view. Not yet.

I knew I needed to just keep climbing. One step at a time.

At the top, fingers trembling, I reached out and pushed the wooden door into the little lookout shelter open. Then I stepped inside. Bear raced into the space after me, immediately settling into a snuggly dog bed that Grandpa had obviously brought up here for him at some point after I left to go home. I smiled, thinking of the two of them sitting up here together, keeping each other company on top of the world.

The lookout shelter was nearly empty; the only furniture inside was Bear's bed and two folding chairs. One for Grandpa . . . and, I suspected, one for me. I had a feeling that, at some point, Grandpa had dragged a chair up all those stairs for me this summer, just in case I ever came up to spend my day at the top, with him.

Cans of Spam lined all the walls, like a weird kind of wallpaper or art installation. There was a small wooden ledge stacked with maps, and the radio I'd used to call in the smoke that day, as well as a few unfamiliar tools and gadgets.

But the most impressive part of the tower was how much I could see from all the way up here: a full 360-degree, bird's-eye view of the forest. I stood in the center of the shelter and spun, gazing out the windows, taking it all in. To the west, evergreen trees intermingled with birch and maple trees that had lost all but the most stubborn of their leaves for the winter. To the east, I had a perfect outlook over the part of the forest that had burned. In time, I knew, the trees would grow back, and life would return.

As I gazed out at the two sides of the forest—both past and future—spread around me, I suddenly heard someone calling my name. I stepped closer to the edge of the shelter and peered out. My breath hitched when I looked down and realized for the first time exactly how far I'd climbed. My sister and Grandpa Howard were at the base of the tower, and they were both calling for me.

I slid open the window and waved. "Up here!" I yelled.

Even from this distance, I could see the surprise on Grandpa's face. Then he smiled and waved back. "Crack a can of Spam; we'll be right up."

AUTHOR'S NOTE

When I was growing up, most of the pictures on my grandparents' walls had a story behind them. The one that always fascinated me most was a photo of my grandpa Howard, nursing a newborn fawn.

The scene in *Controlled Burn* where Maia and Grandpa Howard come upon a dead deer on the side of the road and pull a baby deer from its mother's body was based on a real-life situation. Many years ago, before I was born, my grandpa did exactly that: cut a fawn from its mother's womb, brought it home, and nursed it to good health alongside his dogs—until the deer was old enough to release into a nearby deer park, much like Maia's grandparents did with Wilma.

The idea for *Controlled Burn* has been living as a spark inside me for years. The story has taken time to build and grow, but was ultimately inspired by the event captured in this photo, my own childhood adventures exploring Minnesota's Northwoods and the Boundary Waters Canoe Area with my parents and cousins, Grandpa Howard's stories from his years working in a fire lookout and as a wilderness guide, the peaceful tranquility of the fire tower

and surrounding wilderness outside Tower, MN, and my mom's firsthand experience fighting forest fires in the western United States when I was a kid and teen.

Though my own grandpa Howard was not nearly as gruff as Maia's (my grandpa was hilarious, outgoing, mischievous, and everyone who met him loved him!), so many pieces of his character and Maia's experiences were based on bits and pieces of real life. Grandpa Howard was an adventurer, an explorer, and my hero, but unfortunately, our family lost him to ALS (also known as Lou Gehrig's disease) too soon—when he was just about the age of Maia's grandpa in this story. While writing and planning this novel, I loved having the opportunity to remember and reflect on some of the wonderful time I spent with my amazing grandparents, Howard and Wilma Wagoner, in Minnesota's great Northwoods.

I hope you enjoyed spending time in a place I love so much.

Keep reading for a sneak peak of

JUST KEEP
WALKING

Erin Soderberg Downing

1

The toe of my shoe catches a gnarled tree root. As my foot twists, I quickly jab the tip of my hiking pole into the soft dirt at the edge of the path to stop myself from falling. I take another timid step, testing my ankle on the rugged path.

Sore, not sprained.

Hurt, not broken.

Just keep walking, I tell myself.

I limp on, keeping my eyes on the trail, trying to hold back the tears that are already brimming. I promised myself I wouldn't cry. Especially not on the first day of our hike. And certainly not after what Mom told me a few days ago, when we were pulling the tags and packaging off the last of our new gear. "I better warn you," she'd said, her smile just a weird, wiggly line that made her look like a *Peanuts* character. "I *will* cry when we're out on the trail. Possibly every day."

"Nope, I'm not okay with that," I'd said, shaking my head. "I shouldn't have to deal with a parent crying in front of me. That's not a normal thing to ask."

Mom had laughed, thinking I was being cute. But funny tone or not, I hope she realized I was totally serious. It's weird to watch a parent cry. Wrong. Crying is something to do alone behind closed doors, not out in the open where the whole world can watch you blubber.

"I don't expect you to *do* anything about it, Jo," Mom had added. "Maybe you can just rub my back or give me a hug sometimes. And try to remember that I *want* to be out there with you. I'm the one who offered to do this hike, so that you'd still get to go on your big adventure. I just know I'm going to get overwhelmed. This whole thing is a lot." She'd looked at me seriously. "But even if I start crying, it doesn't mean I want to quit. I need you to remember that, so that maybe you can remind me if I forget."

If Mom's planning to cry on our hike, that means I can't. *Someone* in our party of two needs to keep it together. But with each step, my ankle feels sort of like someone is jabbing it with a hot poker. Maybe I should have gotten hiking *boots*, instead of quick-drying trail *shoes*, but it's a little late for any *shoulda-woulda-couldas* now. I pause, shift my body weight to my hiking poles, roll my foot around in the air, and remind myself to step more carefully from now on. There are going to be a gazillion bumps and roots and rocks ahead, and I'm going to have to figure out how to avoid them.

Just keep walking.

The trail slopes up suddenly, a sharp climb to what the Superior Hiking Trail guidebook promises will be a "rewarding view." My pack pinches my shoulders. The skin on my neck stings. There are thirty pounds of food, gear, and my entire life for two weeks crammed into the turtle shell house I am carrying on my back. Inside the pack, there is a sleeping bag and a thin blow-up sleep pad, the poles for our two-person tent (Mom took the tent and rain fly in her own pack, arguing that she was bigger and should take the extra weight), five dehydrated packaged dinners Mom has promised will be both delicious and nutritious, a tiny folding camp chair, one change of clothes, rain gear, my brother's Swiss Army knife, three water bottles, and a single paperback book that needs to last until we pick up our first food and gear resupply box five days and nearly fifty miles up the trail.

I chose *The Hobbit*.

Because just like Bilbo, I'm setting out on a quest. But unlike Bilbo, mine's not an *unexpected* journey. In fact, I helped plan this adventure. Our trek wasn't sprung on me by a wizard and a pack of dwarves; I *chose* to be here. But as I look ahead at the endless trail of rocks and roots that keeps climbing upward, like a never-ending mountain that's been plopped smack-dab in the middle of mostly flat Minnesota, I can't help but wonder, *why?*

"You holding up okay?" Mom asks, her breath ragged from the climb. "Do you want to lead for a while?"

"No, you can," I tell her. "If I go in front, we're not going to get anywhere fast."

"It's not a race," Mom says. "Want me to walk slower? We have all day."

"This is fine." In time, I'm sure we'll figure out the right speed, who's a better leader and who likes to lag behind, which of us needs a break halfway up each hill and who only stops to rest once they reach the top. My older brother, Jake, told me that's what happened when he and Dad took this same trip together eight years ago. *You have almost two weeks to sort out the kinks*, Jake said with a shrug when I asked him for advice. Just under two weeks, just over one hundred miles. Just a *little* farther than Dad and Jake made it . . . in part, to annoy Dad. In part, to prove we can.

My feet hurt.

My neck stings.

My legs burn.

I already want to quit. But we're going to finish. If we don't, Dad wins. He's already taken enough from us, and I refuse to let him win by thinking we need him around to lead us for stuff like this.

We can do this on our own.

We'll be just fine without him.

Dad's the quitter, not us.

Mom and I walk in silence for a few more minutes, listening to the rustle of birch leaves in the trees overhead. For the past few weeks, I've secretly wondered if we would be stuck chatting about nothing all day—neither Mom nor I do well with awkward silence—or if we'd figure out how to settle into a comfortable quiet. Our house has been a lot quieter lately, especially in those rare times when Mom's gone and I'm home alone. I never used to mind being home by myself. I even *liked* the space and quiet and responsibility of taking care of myself at times. But that was before.

Before Jake went back to college, and before Dad sidestepped into his new family.

After, there were way too many uncomfortable silences. Way too much time to think about before. Now, alone scares me.

Just keep walking.

ACKNOWLEDGMENTS

Special thanks to:

My editor, Sam Palazzi, who is brilliant, insightful, encouraging, and an absolute delight to work with. Reading your notes and thoughts as we revised and polished this book together helped me fall even further in love with this story—which, I think, is the mark of a truly great editor. Also, thanks to David Levithan, who believed in and championed this story at the beginning, and then had the great sense to connect me with Sam. David, I often think about how lucky I am that you took a chance on me all those years ago and taught me almost everything I know about how to craft and perfect a book from the editorial side. You helped shape my career and future in children's books, and now I feel lucky to be working with you on the other side of a manuscript.

My charming, smart, and honest agent, Michael Bourret, who told me after his first read that this story was something special, and then found it the perfect home. Thanks for continuing to stand by my side after a lot of twisty and eventful years, MB.

My mom, Barb Soderberg, for your advice, notes, and endless information on everything having to do with the

BWCA, forest fires, and any general wilderness questions; and also, for sharing lots of memories of and stories about Grandpa Howard. But mostly, thank you for being a huge inspiration and role model for me and so many other girls and women who love the outdoors. You are incredible.

My dad, Kurt Soderberg; Uncle Wayne Dahl; and cousins Lance and Angela Dahl—for all those annual summer canoe-camping trips. Extra-big thanks to Dad, for continuing to explore the woods and lakes and cranberry bogs with me and my kids to this day. We love adventuring with you.

Captain Ben Page, of the Minneapolis Fire Department, for helping with house-fire details and logistics, and answering my questions about what happens after a fire; and Dr. Nils Arvold, who connected me with Dr. Wade Kubat, who advised me on burn care and recovery. (Please note: Though I did a lot of research and asked many questions about both fires and burn aftercare while writing this book, mistakes and inaccuracies are always possible. Any errors are entirely my own fault.)

All the wonderful educators who have connected both me and my books with your students over the years. Thank you for inspiring curiosity and cultivating readers.

The fabulous team at Scholastic, who believed in this book from the very beginning, including Ellie Berger, Kristen Standley, Jana Haussmann, Anna Swenson, Erin Berger, Alan Smagler, and so many more. And the amazing team that helped to make it the best it could possibly be: Melissa Schirmer, Maeve Norton, Jessica White, Courtney Vincento,

Elizabeth Tiffany, the wonderful marketing and publicity teams, and hardworking sales force.

My Minnesota Kid Lit friends and writing buddies (especially Cathy Clark, who sat beside me and cheered during much of the first draft of this story). You guys are magnificent. I'm proud to be part of such a vibrant, encouraging, and supportive community.

Cover artist Oriol Vidal. I have admired your work on so many other books and can't believe I got lucky enough to have you draw my world.

Greg, Milla, Henry, Ruby, Wally, and Meg—for filling my world with love, happiness, and lots of hugs (of the human and doggy variety). You are my everything.

ABOUT THE AUTHOR

Erin Soderberg Downing grew up exploring the forests and lakes of Northern Minnesota, and to this day, her best ideas for stories often come to her deep in the woods, where she can find plenty of creative space to explore and imagine. She has written more than fifty books, including *The Great Peach Experiment* series (a Junior Library Guild Gold Standard Selection), the magical middle-grade novel *Moon Shadow*, and the *Puppy Pirates* chapter book series. Erin currently lives in Minneapolis with her husband, three adventurous kids, and two very fluffy dogs.